WHAT YOU SEE
IS
WHAT YOU HIT

**Your Personal Eyedness, Not Your Personal Handedness
Should Direct You to Your Correct Batting Side**

Good Luck!

Art Kleck

ART KLECK

Fulton Books, Inc.
Meadville, PA

First originally published by Fulton Books 2018

ISBN 978-1-63338-768-3 (Paperback)
ISBN 978-1-63338-769-0 (Digital)

Printed in the United States of America

Warm-Up Time

When and why did you decide you should swing a bat right-handed, or that you should swing a bat left-handed? Were you coached by a hitting wizard like Stan Musial, Ernie Banks, Ted Williams, or Jackie Robinson? Perhaps by Ty Cobb, Babe Ruth, Willie Mays, or Yogi Berra? My guess is that very few of you had that opportunity. And even if you had the chance to get their advice, how much would you have gained from it?

Chances are better that it was your mom or dad or sister or brother or a friend who showed you how to bat and perhaps even suggested that you should bat right-handed if you are a right-handed person and left-handed if you are a left-handed person. Or perhaps you just picked up a bat when you were six or seven and decided then and there that you'd bat right-handed because that felt comfortable and also most of the older kids batted that way. Let's think about it. How scientific was this whole process?

However and whenever you made your decision on which way to swing a bat, you undoubtedly left out the most important factor. That key factor? Are you right-eye dominant or are you left-eye dominant? That's what this book is all about. I hope to prove to you that it is eye dominance or eyedness only that should really determine which way each person should swing a bat to achieve his or her greatest success. I contend that one must bat from one's personal correct eyedness side to see and hit the ball with maximum success.

Why not risk the possibility that you may have made a child-hood mistake? Examine carefully what I have to say in these pages and then make a sound scientific decision based on your personal,

3

specific, ocular dominance. If you made the correct decision early, just keep doing it that way. If you made a wrong decision, be willing and eager to change your batting side now. Whether you bat right-handed or left-handed should depend on your personal eye dominance. It should not depend on whether you are right-handed or left-handed. So far as I know or can determine from some research done, nobody else has put himself out on a limb to make this declaration. I feel very comfortable out on this limb. I am very firm in my belief that the facts of science are all on my side. I contend that it is each individual's, either right- or left-eye dominance, only that should be the deciding factor in telling each person which way to bat.

Soon I'll put you through an easy vision test that will inform you scientifically whether you are right-eyed or left-eyed or equal-eyed or flip-flop-eyed. Then I'll help you determine which batters' box will be most friendly to you. I hope I've aroused your curiosity. Let's get on with it.

Here are some of the random and casual observations I've made over the many years I've observed and tested people for their ocular dominance or eyedness. I prefer to call this "random investigation" rather than even pretend that it meets the standards of "scientific research." The research done by others on ocular dominance to this point in history does not convince me that I am incorrect. The figures listed below are results derived from my random testing of approximately eight thousand people over a period of sixty-five years for their specific eyedness or eye dominance.

Approximately 95 percent of people are either right-eye dominant (right-eyed) or left-eye dominant (left-eyed).

Approximately 1 percent of people are equal-eye dominant (equal-eyed).

Approximately 4 percent of people are flip-flop-eye dominant (flip-flop-eyed). This category of people can be right-eye dominant one moment and left-eye dominant the next moment depending on that person's item of focus. Only one of the people I've tested in this category enjoyed the challenge of a baseball or softball coming toward them.

I have personally chosen the word *flip-flop* to describe this condition. None of the research I've reviewed addresses this confusing condition. I really have no helpful hitting suggestions for this group of people.

On a spring day in 1948, following a physics class discussion on optics, focal distances, microscopes, and telescopes, Mr. Farber and I had an after class discussion. We talked about eye dominance or eyedness. I was instantly fascinated by the subject. Following that discussion with my very favorite teacher that day in 1948, I began to toy with the idea that baseball and fast-pitch softball players should bat from the side of the plate that their eyedness, not their handedness, directs. That theory boiled with greater intensity as I aged and my experiences supporting this theory also multiplied. Then that enthusiastic encouragement from, Stan Musial in 1954, "to write my book." Stan Musial has been a powerful influence.

One of my favorite friends said to me recently, "Art, now that you are eighty-four, why don't you write that book you've been thinking about for several years? Odds are you don't have many decades left to do it." Yes, the years pass quickly.

My special thanks to the many great kids at our annual Kleck family reunions held each June at Archbold, Ohio's beautiful Ruihley Park. I plan to continue throwing Wiffle balls to you kids for several more years. My past experiences of throwing Wiffle balls to you, and casually testing you for your eye dominance, has been fun and scientifically enlightening. These annual experiences have provided a key factor of encouragement to me to write this book.

Dale Quillet was my excellent high school varsity baseball catcher. Every successful pitcher really needs a catcher who is willing to be in charge defensively, a catcher who can effectively handle low or wide pitches, and a catcher who can throw hard and accurately to first, second, or third base to catch a runner off base. Dale Quillet gets high marks here.

Don Kleck, my wonderful brother who is four years younger than I am, was my helpful practice catcher during the summer months of 1948 through 1952. For at least thirty minutes of each summer day, he and I would play pitch and catch in our driveway. He was the perfect brother. He took lots of hits to the chins on low pitches, but he never complained. He just offered constant encouragement to get my pitches up another foot so they'd be called strikes.

My very special thanks to my lovely wife, Barbara, who provided her continuing encouragement to write this book. She knew, better than anyone else, that I am really convinced that I have an idea and a discovery based on experience that must be shared with others.

And a very emphatic thank you to Patricia de la Mora, a very positive and intelligent former bookstore manager. She tirelessly transcribed my sometimes difficult to read handwritten manuscript and cheered me on to the finish line with her undiminished encouragement and patience. Thank you. Thank you all!

My Target Readers

1. Baseball players—all levels (Little League through professional)
2. Fast-pitch softball players—all levels
3. Baseball coaches—all levels
4. Fast-pitch softball coaches—all levels
5. Parents who want to get their kids off to safe and successful batting start
6. Baseball managers—professional
7. Major league team owners
8. College and major league baseball scouts
9. Athletic directors—high school and college
10. Golfers, especially those who are swinging from their incorrect side now
11. Golf and other sports equipment sales people
12. Coaches and players of all competitive sports
13. Firearms sales people and the sportsmen and policemen using firearms
14. Highway safety engineers and other people involved in the design of roadways and entry roads to highways.
15. Automotive engineers
16. Automobile drivers and truck drivers
17. Elementary school safety planners and teachers
18. Assembly line designers and owners of manufacturing plants

First Inning

What I am proposing in these pages is scientifically sound and makes the games of baseball and fast-pitch softball more fun for both players and spectators. Understanding exactly what it takes to see each pitch most accurately is what I strive to achieve. When the batter sees the pitch very accurately, hitting the pitch squarely becomes an easier task. Perhaps even some of you golfers and cricket players will want to consider swinging from the other side after you have examined what I have to say.

I hope to convince you that the correct batting side for each person should depend on each person's eye dominance. That correct batting side should not depend on whether you are right-handed or left-handed. Each person's correct batting side should be determined only by each individual's right or left-eye dominance.

Ninety-five percent of people possess one eye that is constantly more dominant than the other. You will perform a test during the second inning that will prove to you whether you are right-eye dominant (right-eyed) or whether you are left-eye dominant (left-eyed). If you are right-eye dominant, as 75 to 80 percent of people are, then you should bat left-handed. If you are left-eye dominant, as about 15 to 20 percent of people are, then you should bat right-handed. I cannot make a recommendation to the 4 percent of our population who are flip-flop-eyed. These people will just have to figure out which side works best for each of them. I have estimated, that through my lifetime of casually testing people to determine their eyedness or eye dominance, that approximately 45 percent of little league, high school, and college baseball and fast-pitch softball players are swinging a bat from the incorrect side today.

In the following pages, I will deal primarily with baseball and fast-pitch softball, sports that require the two-handed swing from either the right or left-hand batter's box. The very important factors here are the two-handed side-on-swing and the individual batter's eye dominance or eyedness.

Handedness is a human attribute defined by unequal distribution of motor skills between the right and left hands in each of us. An individual who is more dexterous with the right hand is called "right-handed" and one more dexterous with the left hand is called "left-handed." Less than 1 percent of humans are ambidextrous where both right and left hands are equally skilled at performing similar tasks.

My own personal observations as a teacher, coach, and high school principal suggests that about 90 percent of people are right-handed, leaving about 10 percent left-handed and less than 1 percent ambidextrous.

Likewise about 95 percent of people possess one eye more constantly dominant than the other. This can be referred to as ocular dominance or eyedness. Most right-handed people are also right-eye dominant and most left-handed people are left-eye dominant. Even though this pattern exists, it has been clear to me for many years that each person must be individually tested to determine each person's eye dominance before choosing the better batting side.

Both left-eyed and right-eyed people perform on a very equal basis in performing the normal activities of each day. One is not better than the other in any way; just as left-handed people and right-handed people are very equal in their performance in all tasks. Both hands functioning well makes it easy for us to perform tasks that require the use of both hands. Likewise, both eyes functioning well makes it easy for us to perform tasks that require the use of both eyes for maximum vision.

If you want to read a book based on very technical scientific research, don't read my book. If you want to read a book based on real life experiences and good science helping you reach a solid common sense conclusion, please read my book. I really think you'll like it. I know you'll gain some insights into swinging the bat from the correct side of the plate, and maybe even offer some very constructive assistance to those who are swinging from the incorrect side now.

Some, but not enough good scientific research, has been done in recent years regarding ocular dominance. None that I have explored diminishes my very strong conviction that I am correct regarding the "side-on-swing" in baseball and fast-pitch softball. That is, for best hitting success each player's eyedness or ocular dominance should direct the player to the correct batting side. The player's handedness should not play a role in this decision.

I have found some correct answers through my long-term experiences and observations with my emphasis primarily on hitting a baseball and softball. In this book, I have also touched on many other facets of our lives that are affected by our personal ocular dominance.

I want to emphasize that many of you are already swinging from the correct side and should simply continue this good process. For the rest of you, who will learn as a result of taking the upcoming eye dominance test, that you are presently swinging from the incorrect side. Just face it squarely and make the change. This eye test is outlined during the second inning just ahead. If your playing days are behind you, please take the time to help a younger person discover his or her correct side. You'll see and feel immediate improvement in both seeing and hitting the ball from your correct side. Just do it. It works.

It really doesn't matter at all what the percentages of right-eyed versus left-eyed people in this world. All that really matters is: What is your personal eyedness or ocular dominance, and therefore, from which side of the plate should you swing the bat for maximum effectiveness? When you swing from the correct side, you swing more smoothly, more comfortably, more safely and more accurately for a much higher batting average. It really works.

It is really the "side-on-swing" that really presents the challenge to one's eyes. Even though the "side-on-swing" is also used in cricket, golf, and hockey, I have elected to stick with baseball and fast-pitch softball where I possess the proper knowledge and life experiences. I contend, however, that these other sport athletes can pick up some valuable tips here. Yes, even football and soccer players can get some good tips. Since 95 percent of people possess one eye dominant over the other, we should, each one of us, determine which eye we can count on for reliable and truthful information. Which eye is this in your case? I'll help you determine that fact with a very simple test as we move along.

Please understand from the outset, I am not stating or suggesting that 95 percent of us have one good eye and one bad eye. Far from that. Rather, our right eye and left eye work together in beautiful concert with our brain to give us the spectacular God-given gift of sight.

Just as one of our hands is usually more capable than the other in performing the simple act of writing legibly, one of our eyes is more capable than the other in providing very accurate positional information regarding the objects we see. Eyes and brain work together to accomplish this. The player must see the ball very accurately to hit it very successfully.

I base my observations, suggestions, and conclusions not on the basis of research already done, nor on any in-depth research done by me, but rather on the lack of excellent and convincing research that in any way refutes my hypothesis.

There has been substantial research done on ocular dominance, but none of it convinces me that my hypothesis is incorrect regarding the "side-on-swing." The word *hypothesis*, as defined in the American Heritage Dictionary by the Houghton Mifflin Company is as follows: Hypothesis—"An explanation that accounts for a set of facts that can be tested by further investigation."

My hypothesis simply stated is: "For maximum success, right-eyed or right-eye dominant baseball and fast-pitch softball players should swing a bat left-handed; that is, from the left-hand batter's box nearest first base. Likewise, for maximum success, left-eyed or left-eye dominant players should swing a bat right-handed; that is, from the right-hand batter's box nearest third base."

The time has come in my life that I feel immensely compelled to share my thoughts and ideas with you for your genuine consideration and personal examination. I am confident that you will derive some personal benefits. Maybe you will even use some of what you learn here for personal profit. I hope so. The ideas and concepts I'm sharing with you here have scientific ramifications well beyond the sports of baseball and softball. I'll touch on some of this as I pace you through these pages. I am eager for each of you readers to think about and develop your own ideas as to how this "eye science" can be applied in other facets of our lives. It's the teacher in me that encourages you to challenge yourselves to invent something useful for others using this information.

If you or a friend have ever worked on an assembly line, that moving assembly line has usually moved from workers' left to workers' right. I have found this to be the actual case in the various assembly plants I've checked. Since 75 to 80 percent of humans are right-eyed or right-eye dominant, most of the assembly line workers would see the objects more precisely if the assembly line moved from right to left. That could certainly improve worker efficiency, comfort, and safety.

Should our entry lanes to major multiple-lane highways be on the left instead of the right side as they are now in the United States? In Great Britain and Ireland, the entry lanes are usually on the left. Perhaps they are doing this correctly. Maybe their highway engineers have applied eye science as I am in this book. They also drive on the left side of the roadway and experience many fewer accidents per miles driven than we in the United States. We should study this carefully. Should highway engineers study this more carefully? Could we save thousands of accidents and lives if we made this change? We could easily adjust to a monumental change for great improvement of safety for ourselves and our children.

During the twelve years I was the principal of Lake Forest High School's West Campus, I had reasons to meet with the Lake Forest police chief at least once each year. Chief Charles Gilbert was a highly respected and excellent chief. Our relationship with the police department was very positive. Community administration, police department, fire department, and school administration worked together very harmoniously for the great good of our citizens in Lake Forest, Illinois.

On one occasion when I met with our police chief, Charlie Gilbert, he commented to me prior to our regular meeting, that he had just returned from a traffic safety meeting in one of the adjacent suburbs where a very interesting discussion had centered on the fact that our United States auto accident rate per miles driven had far exceeded the accident rate experienced in Great Britain. He said most of the officers at that meeting were astounded at that fact. He noted that in Great Britain, one drives on the left side of the road. Most officers at the meeting agreed that this didn't appear to be as safe to them as driving on the right side of the road as we do it in the United States.

I surprised my friend, Charles Gilbert, when I quickly stated that "I thought the British got it right whenever they decided to drive on the left side of the road." I then gave Charles Gilbert the eyedness test. He was both right-handed and right-eyed. I don't remember ever discussing the subject of eyedness with Chief Gilbert again. I really think that the English got it right. Since I have found that 75 to 80 percent of the human population is right-eyed, this makes great sense to me. What do you think?

I hope to convince you of the good logic and common sense of *What You See Is What You Hit* through my experiences, my testing of others, and my observations over many years. Add to this my keen interest and involvement, first as a baseball and fast-pitch softball player through high school, and college days, followed by many years of teaching science and coaching baseball, football, tennis, and basketball at the high school level and my continuing interest in sports.

Second Inning

In the summer of 1954, I had a very interesting and convincing conversation with Stan Musial, the very famous Hall of Fame baseball player with the St. Louis Cardinals.

I had been drafted into the United States Army four days following my graduation from Denison University in June of 1953. I was stationed at Ft. Leonard Wood, Missouri, a United States Army base located about a three-hour drive from the old St. Louis Cardinal baseball stadium, Sportsmans' Park. In those days, the St. Louis Cardinals of the National League and the old St. Louis Browns of the American League shared this stadium as a home park for each.

Photo taken: June 30, 1953
Fort Leonard Wood, MO
Art Kleck - 1953

The Korean War ended shortly after I entered the service, but we draftees were required to remain in the service for our full two years. I enjoyed my military service time and gained much from that experience.

Three of my army buddies and I went to a St. Louis Cardinal baseball game on a beautiful 1954 summer day. The Cardinal management gave us complimentary stadium passes since we were military service people and wearing our official uniforms. Military service pay was only about $65 per month in those days. We loved the free passes.

After Stan Musial completed his pregame batting practice that day, he came over to us and with a big smile said to my buddies and me, "Thanks for serving, soldiers. I'd like to sign your score cards." He was a very relaxed and cordial person. I asked him if he'd talk with me for just a few minutes. I explained to him very briefly that one of my present army duties was to provide a class lecture and discussion each Monday morning for two hundred military policemen. Bringing the troops up to date on national, international, and sports news was my challenge. Reporting on sports was really the most fun for me. Stan Musial said, "I'll try to answer any questions you have, soldier." In just the next five minutes, the great warmth and kindness of Stan Musial's character really dominated.

On that beautiful sunny day I had the very happy opportunity of testing my all-time favorite baseball player concerning his eye dominance. I started my conversation with Stan Musial by asking him if he had ever tried batting right-handed. He smiled broadly and answered, "Soldier, I've tried that in the past. I just couldn't see the ball very well when I tried batting right-handed. I just gave up trying to hit the ball right-handed and ever since I've been with the St. Louis Cardinals I've batted left-handed against all pitchers."

I then asked him if he would mind performing an eye test for me right then to determine his eye dominance or eyedness. Even without doing the test, I had guessed that this very splendid .331 lifetime left-handed hitter just had to be right-eyed. He repeated the test three times in the next three minutes and proved to himself and to me that he was, for sure, right-eye dominant or right-eyed.

He then smiled broadly and said, "I think I now finally understand why I just couldn't hit the ball right-handed. Soldier, you'd better write a book about that stuff. You can be sure that I'll always bat left-handed. Now don't you forget to write that book."

The St. Louis Cardinals won the game that day in 1954. Stan Musial had either two or three hits in four times at bat. He continued to bat left-handed for his entire career. Stan Musial was right-eyed.

The test that day proved it to himself and to me. When I told Stan Musial that I was surprised to see him sign autographs right-handed he just smiled and said," I just do that to keep all the parts working." What a nice man and how very cordial with his fans. He will likely be known as "The Pride of St. Louis" for many years to come.

I have observed through decades of carefully following major league baseball that St. Louis Cardinal fans are loyal, extremely loyal. Those fans are proud to claim Stan Musial as a favorite son. He was greatly admired by opponents' players, as well as by his teammates. When he hit a home run, there was no "showboating" as he rounded the bases. Opposing pitchers, and players, and all fans always appreciated his sportsmanship style.

For the balance of the game that day in 1954, my buddies and I watched Stan Musial very closely. After all, he had taken the time to be very friendly with us. It was almost as if we, each one of us, had a new friend who was already very famous in the sports world. He even waved to us twice after the game got underway. My buddies and I observed that sometimes between innings that day Stan Musial actually appeared to be giving that eye test to some of his teammates. This helped convince me that Stan Musial was very serious when he said, "Soldier, you'd better write a book about that stuff."

Stan Musial won seven National League batting titles, was the National League's Most Valuable Player (MVP) three times, and was a twenty-four time all-star during his twenty-two years with the St. Louis Cardinals. During some of his years in the major leagues, two all-star games were played each year. Stan Musial was inducted into the Baseball Hall of Fame in 1969, his first year of eligibility.

More than sixty years have passed since that very special day in 1954 when Stan Musial encouraged me to write this book. My only regret is that I did not get it written while Stan Musial was living. I think he would have liked it.

I'd like to suggest to all good baseball fans that you visit the Cooperstown Baseball Hall of Fame. I've visited the Cooperstown Baseball Hall of Fame three times and will probably return again. Important details regarding each inducted player are clearly stated on each player's bronze plaque. If you have a great interest in baseball and baseball history, I urge you to make this trip to the Cooperstown Baseball Hall of Fame in New York State.

Stan Musial served about fourteen months in the United States Navy during and right after World War II. He did not play any part of the 1945 baseball season with the St. Louis Cardinals during his United States Navy service time.

More than four hundred major league players served our country in one of our military services during World War II. President Franklin D. Roosevelt strongly supported the fact that major league baseball should continue during that World War II, but did not permit avoiding the draft into service for any of the players for the reason of playing major league baseball, a good and fair decision by a great president. I was extremely happy that major league baseball could continue during that very strenuous time in our United States history. I was an avid baseball fan. The news of the ongoing war was often very sad and the news of Major League baseball was mostly enjoyable.

The Eye Dominance Test

Now let's all do the eye dominance test that Stan Musial took that day at the St. Louis Cardinal ballpark. The purpose of this test is to determine which one of your eyes is dominant and therefore tells you the "complete truth" regarding the location and speed of the object you see.

1. Please have a friend read the directions to you as you perform the test yourself. Repeat the test three times to confirm that you've done the test properly and that you've gotten consistent results.
2. Now facing straight ahead and with both arms down at your sides and with both eyes wide open, look at a small object at least twenty to thirty feet away and directly in front of you and at least five feet off the floor.

3. The object could be one hundred or more feet away.

4. With your left arm extended in front of you, point at the selected object with your left index finger,

5. Keeping both eyes wide open as you point, that left index finger will likely appear somewhat transparent.

6. Now with your right hand, cover your right eye. Keep your left index finger steady on the target. Do not turn your head nor move that pointing finger.

7. Where are you pointing now? If you appear to be pointing one to three feet to the right of the target and a bit lower than the target, you are probably right-eye dominant or right-eyed. Now cover your left eye only. If your pointing finger is back on the target, you are for sure right-eye dominant.

8. Keep your left index finger steady on the target with both eyes wide open again. Now cover your left eye with your right hand. Do not move your pointing finger. Where are you pointing now? If you appear to be pointing one to three feet to the left of the target you are probably left-eye dominant or left-eyed. Now cover your right eye only. If your pointing finger moves back to the target, you are for sure left-eyed.

9. If your pointing finger does not appear to move off the target as you cover first right, then left eye, you are then equal-eye dominant or equal-eyed. Only 1 percent of people are equal-eyed. If you are equal-eyed, you could probably swing the bat equally well right or left-handed.

10. There is another small percentage of the many people I've tested over the years, about 4 percent, whose eye dominance skips back and forth from right-eye dominance to left-eye dominance, depending on that person's object of focus. Example: If this person covers the right eye while taking the test, the pointing finger moves to the lower right of the target. If the same person covers the left eye, the pointing finger moves to the lower left of the target. Let's call this condi-

tion flip-flop dominance or flip-flop-eyedness. Of the many people I've tested over the years since 1948, only about 4 percent had this condition. Of this small number, most had never played baseball or fast-pitch softball. Some of this group even noted that they are "highly challenged" when objects are coming toward them, as one object can appear to be two and two objects can appear to be four. A few of them noted that driving a car presents genuine challenges to them. I've not found many active or former baseball or softball players with this flip-flop-eyedness condition. Tommy Myers is a notable exception. Very logically, there are many.

11. Now do the test over two or three times to make sure you've got it correctly.
12. Next, read the directions to your friend and have the friend take the test.

I suggest at this point that you and your friend discuss and comment on the test you've just taken. Is it beginning to make great sense to you that each batter's eye dominance should determine the correct side swing?

I've given this very simple ocular dominance test to approximately eight thousand people since that memorable day in my high school physics class in 1948. I don't pretend to call this process academic research. I prefer to call it casual and random information gathering and idea enhancement over a period of sixty-five years.

During the many years I taught both the physical and biological sciences, I frequently administered the eye dominance test to twenty-five students simultaneously. Add to this, many times when I've tested eight to ten friends or fellow teachers at social gatherings. There have also been some periods of time when I've tested nobody for a month. During my twelve years of coaching high school sports, many of my student athletes took the eye dominance test. Most of the people who have taken the test through the years have been intrigued with their personal results. The test is usually a great conversation starter.

Now let's talk about Tommy Myers, the flip-flop-eyed guy who has proven his excellence as a hitter and all-around athlete, teacher, and coach. He is the exception I noted when you took the eye dominance test.

Tommy graduated from Lake Forest High School in 1966. During his years at Lake Forest High School in Illinois, Tommy was a star athlete in baseball, basketball, and football. Second base, point guard, and quarterback were team positions he played with great excellence. He always played smart and with maximum effort. It was truly fun to watch Tommy play each game. He was a "team player" always and a highly respected leader.

Then off to Albion College in Michigan where he, again, was a baseball and football star. In his senior year at Albion, Tommy was selected First Team Second Baseman All-Conference, Michigan Intercollegiate Athletic Association.

After graduation from Albion College, Tommy continued to play semi-pro baseball in the Shoreline and other leagues in Illinois until he was forty-two years old. He did lots of switch-hitting after graduation from college. Through all the years beginning with high school days through age forty-two, Tommy kept his hitting average very close to .333 for all seasons. His fielding was always nearly flawless too.

I had the good fortune to hire Tommy Myers while I was the principal at Lake Forest West Campus High School. He taught physical education and coached baseball, basketball, and football at Lake Forest High School for the next thirty-five years. Our students were richly blessed to have this truly outstanding person as their teacher, mentor, coach, and role model.

He still coaches football at Lake Forest College in 2017. His very positive influence runs deep in these communities. He's a person you'd like to know.

Flip-flop-eyedness has never been a deficit for Tommy Myers, but I remind you that all other people I've interviewed with this condition have found it to be a handicap so far as seeing and hitting a pitched baseball or softball is concerned.

Third Inning

Now that you know your eye dominance, as a result of the test, do a few pretend practice swings from your correct side. This may seem uncoordinated at first if this is not the way you've always swung the bat. However, you'll be impressed by how rapidly swinging from the correct side becomes easy and natural. Pick up a bat this spring at your first opportunity and start practicing your correct side swing. Help others too. You will be delighted with the results after you have practiced, practiced, practiced hitting either Wiffle balls in your backyard or hitting baseballs or softballs at the high school batting cage or at a regular baseball field, always taking the full swing or bunting from the correct side of the plate.

I have found that using Wiffle balls can be a great idea. They are very safe too. Even if you get hit by a wild pitch from your brother, sister, dad, or friend, it won't really hurt. It gives you the confidence to just stand in the batter's box and concentrate on hitting the ball.

Another great advantage of using Wiffle balls is that one can also purchase Waffle balls that are slotted on one hemisphere. These balls make it very simple for anyone to throw a hard breaking or gently breaking curveball or screwball. Just follow the directions on the package. The slotted ball will break in the direction the slots are facing. The slots cause additional air friction, thereby pulling the ball in the direction of greater air friction. This requires no pitching skill. Just hold the ball per directions on the package. Throw it with your normal throwing motion.

The more common wiffle ball is uniformly perforated. This ball will travel in a reasonably straight line path to the batter. Mix them up, just as a good pitcher mixes curves, changeups, screwballs, sliders, and fastballs. You need only a modestly sized backyard to do the Wiffle ball practice.

Please understand, there is really no need to go through the Wiffle ball stage in becoming skilled at hitting from your correct side. Do it with regulation baseballs on a baseball diamond or in a batting cage from the outset if you wish. I, however, encourage using Wiffle balls for all kids under twelve as they change to a new batters' box side. Their new correct side swing will probably require three hundred practice swings before the new correct side swing feels comfortable. Please don't be surprised, however, if the superior athletes among you will feel very comfortable swinging from the newly discovered correct side after just seventy to eighty swings. This book is all about finding your correct side swing so you can quickly see the ball better with your "truth telling" eye nearest the pitcher.

Those of you who started swinging from the correct side early have great advantage over the number of kids who began and continued to swing from the incorrect side. However, those of you who are moderately good to excellent athletes should have no difficulty making the proper switch to the correct side. Yes, you'll have to put in some good practice time. Any athlete in any sport who really wants to improve needs to practice. The more you practice, the luckier you'll get.

While I was the West Campus Lake Forest high school principal in Lake Forest, Illinois, from July 1971 through July 1983, I had this framed print on the wall behind my desk. I consider this a worthwhile thought for all people to ponder. The noted Roman philosopher, Seneca wrote this in 4 B.C.

Luck
is what happens
when
preparation
meets
opportunity.

The great golfer, Ben Hogan, was once asked by a sports writer, "How can you be so lucky as to get off so many great shots?"

Ben Hogan replied, "The more I practice, the luckier I get." I am quite confident that Ben Hogan hit golf balls from his correct side. I think this note can easily apply to many facets of our lives. Athletes who practice most diligently and condition themselves most correctly will be luckier than others. Business people who prepare more diligently will be luckier than others. Batters who practice diligently from the correct side will be luckier than those who swing from the incorrect side. Perhaps in all facets of our lives we should place ourselves on the "correct side" and then practice whatever we do with great conviction.

During my high school years I was a four-year varsity starting baseball player. I played third base, second base, and center field during my freshman and sophomore years. I was my school's number one starting pitcher during my junior and senior years. On days when I could not pitch, I continued to play center field or third base.

I played three years of varsity baseball at Denison University. During my junior and senior years, I was my team's number one starting pitcher. Through all of my high school and college years, I also played fast-pitch softball during the summer months.

I've played very little golf, and during the ten years I played golf, between 1960 and 1970, I was an absolutely incompetent golfer. I now know why I played so poorly on all occasions. I kept trying to hit the ball from the wrong side. Since I am a right-hander, I quickly concluded that I should buy right-handed golf clubs. The golf pro at the golf course where I bought the clubs urged me to buy them. He said, "All right-handers should swing right-handed." I had turned age thirty just two months prior to buying those new golf clubs. I certainly couldn't blame old clubs for my very poor golf performances. Once a golfer has right-handed clubs, it is really not easy to experiment hitting left-handed. In those days I didn't even focus on the fact that I am right-eyed. Now I know that I should have at least experimented with a left-handed driver. I just wasn't thinking logically.

I simply could not hit golf balls well or consistently with those right-handed clubs. I couldn't keep my head down either, as many golfing friends had encouraged me to do.

I haven't played golf in forty-six years since I gave my very slightly used right-handed clubs to a friend. He has claimed little golfing success either. When I tested him twenty years later, he proved to be right-eyed also.

I bought a new left-handed driver a few months ago. I wanted to test my hypothesis on myself one more time. I also bought a bucket of forty golf-ball-sized Wiffle balls. Now I'm enjoying a new golf ball hitting experience with those Wiffle balls and my new left-handed driver. It is fun for me, hitting most of the balls squarely, left-handed.

I really don't plan to play golf again, but I will for sure, go to the driving range a few times. I will swing left-handed with my new left-handed driver. I will also continue to hit Wiffle balls left-handed in our backyard. It makes me smile.

By the way, I don't think I'm keeping my head down very much. It's just easy for me to see the golf ball and hit it with this left-handed driver. I'm hitting from my correct side now. I seriously doubt that it is my two recent knee replacements that have made it easier for me to hit those golf balls left-handed.

I'd like to suggest to golfers that you buy a driver for your golf bag with a face different from all the others you now carry. Also try the new driver a few times at the driving range. Who knows, it may become very friendly to you. It will also become very helpful when you get stuck behind a rock or tree and your regular clubs just won't bail you out.

Let's review some simple and very important facts. Ninety-five percent of people possess one eye that is more dominant than the other. That is the "truth telling eye" working with the brain to give us reliable information concerning the things we see and the exact location of the things we see. This is a massive oversimplification of the beautiful process called sight.

The complexities of sight are amazing to study and attempt to understand. Sight is truly a wonderful miracle of nature, one of God's many incredible gifts to us.

The two-handed side-on-swing is a complex movement that must be kept in sync with eye dominance or eyedness for the ultimate swinging success. The important third ingredient is the pitched ball moving toward the batter. Timing, accuracy, restrictive, and fluid movement are all part of the total process and much easier to accomplish from the correct side of the plate. It also becomes more natural and fun that way.

The major problem has been that many of us grew up swinging from the incorrect side. Changing all of this now may seem too much for us to correct. To the contrary, I think you'll find it both fun and rewarding. It really isn't too difficult to change this bad habit. Once you establish which is your correct side, just practice it that way and be confident that you are now doing it the correct way. It gets easier with each swing and the results are very rewarding. As I pointed out earlier, approximately 80 to 85 percent of all right-handed people are also right-eyed and should therefore swing left-handed. Likewise, approximately 80 to 85 percent of left-handed people are left-eyed and should, therefore, swing right-handed. My uncomplicated definition of a right-hander is "a person who throws a ball best and writes best right-handed." Likewise, a left-hander is "a person who throws a ball best and writes best left-handed."

Still other important factors to consider in the two-handed side-on-swing are hand and arm strength and coordination. I will incorporate all of these factors as we move forward in the process. I will make all of this very easy to understand.

I certainly don't want to suggest that we produce more switch-hitters. Far from that, I am suggesting that we produce more skilled swingers from the correct side. Have you heard of a single time when Stan Musial or Ted Williams or Yogi Berra batted right-handed during their star-studded major league careers? These three great players batted left-handed every time. We also know for sure that Stan Musial was right-eyed. Though I don't know for sure, it is a pretty safe bet that Yogi Berra was right-eyed also. Yogi Berra was an excellent Yankee catcher who threw the ball right-handed. His power hand was at the knob of the bat.

I hope you've had the opportunity to observe in person or on film the beautiful smooth swings of each of these great athletes. Later on, I'll talk more about the power hand and the guide hand as they relate to successful swinging from the correct side.

Only 1 percent of humans are equal-eyed. This should be a very desirable circumstance for a middle linebacker on a football team or a center fielder in baseball or softball or a very talented playmaker and leading assist basketball player. Stan Musial tested Ted Williams at an All-Star game and discovered that Ted Williams was equal-eyed. He had no blind spots. He also had his power hand at the knob of the bat. Ted Williams threw the ball right-handed. He was a fabulous left-handed hitter.

The great assist and playmaker talents of Joakim Noah of the 2014 Chicago Bulls indicate that he is probably equal-eye dominant. His great talent as an assist specialist, and as a key playmaker certainly suggest this. In any event, his talents as a basketball playmaker are immense. Equal-eyed people possess no blind spots.

Was Mickey Mantle equal-eyed? I do not know. I know he hit the ball equally well from either side of the plate and was a very accomplished center fielder for the New York Yankees. Both Mickey Mantle and the fabulous Joe DiMaggio who preceded Mantle in the Yankee center field position may have been equal-eyed. Their fielding skills indicated this, but we'll never know their eyedness for sure.

I suggest that very young children be taken to an eye doctor, an oculist, at a very early age, not only to carefully check the child's eye health, but also to learn the child's eye dominance. I've learned through my career in high school education as a teacher, coach, and principal that many young people don't get an eye health exam by a well-trained oculist (eye doctor) until they have sight problems. Thorough early eye exams scheduled by thoughtful parents for their children could help prevent many later sight problems. The oculist can inform the parents at the conclusion of the exam concerning the eye dominance of each child. Then it should be the parents' responsibility to assist the child in swinging from the correct side.

I do not advocate forcing a child to swing a bat or golf club from the correct side if the child shows great discomfort or resistance. Maybe the child has little or no interest in hitting a ball. Most children will reach their own point of readiness to try a sport. They'll all need help or guidance when they show that interest. I prefer to get them started correctly whenever that time arrives.

Robbie Bugbee - 2014

Later in this book, I talk about Grandma Jan as she tosses the nerf ball to little Robbie at the age of three and how Robbie smacks each nerf ball back to Grandma Jan using his little plastic bat. That's the same Robbie that really captured my intense interest as he hit line drives back to me as I pitched Wiffle balls to him in later years at our annual family reunions. He's an excellent hitter today. He bats right-handed and is left-eye dominant. He is batting exceptionally well at age eighteen. He is batting from his correct side.

Robbie Bugbee is also a very accomplished high school lacrosse player, one of the very best in the state of North Carolina. Lacrosse is a sport that is highly dependent on eye-hand coordination. Now his left-eyedness and his right-handedness are assets to him as he excels in the fast moving sport of lacrosse.

It is my guess that most of today's major league star hitters are hitting from their correct sides. But how many more star hitters would exist if some of the very average major league hitters and other baseball players would hit from their correct sides also? We won't know until each player determines his or her dominant eye and then, if not swinging from the correct side, gives the correct side a try with reasonable practice to support the switch.

I've learned that most players who are switch-hitters became switch-hitters simply because they felt too challenged by pitches moving away from them like the curveball or slider. Switch-hitters usually bat left-handed against right-handed pitchers and right-handed against left-handed pitchers to avoid trying to hit the challenging "breakaway pitch."

I would like to suggest to switch-hitters that they give my recommended strategy a good try. Simply swing from the correct side against all pitchers. This approach can also be a tremendous confidence builder for the hitter. The hitter is, in effect, telling the pitcher; throw me any pitch in your repertoire, I can see and hit them all. All pitches can be seen and timed more precisely from the correct side. The dominant eye, when closest to the pitcher, conveys more accurate positional and speed information regarding each pitch.

Art Kleck on a practice day at Denison U. on May 10, 1953

Left   Right
Don Alt and Art Kleck
Baseball Co-Captains (1953)
with Coach Kieth Piper

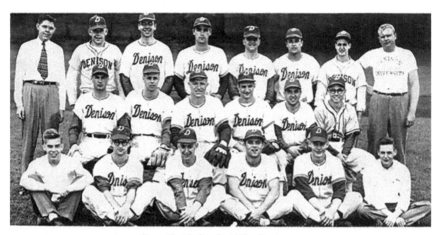

1st row—Stevens, Vogt, Fordyce, Ryno, Kelley, Simmons.
2nd row—Brown, McKenney, Kleck, Alt, Jochens, Davis.
3rd row—Neale, Cook, Wade, Cash, Ward, Bowen, Thomas, Piper.

BASEBALL

Bob Vogt demonstrates his winning batting stance. Vogt led the powerful Big Red stickmen with a .395 total.

Keith Piper's second years as coach of the Denison baseball team was a very successful one as his squad won eight games out of twelve. Their Ohio Conference record was seven wins against three losses, good enough to tie for first place in the Conference. This constitutes the best record the Big Red diamond men have accumulated in ten years. Very stable pitching and good hitting paced the Big Red in their wins, and loose fielding accounted for the losses.

Art Kleck initiated the season with a five hit whitewash of Wittenberg, 3-0. Sam McKenney's relief hurling and a big nine-run sixth inning downed Wooster 20-8. After defeating Lockbourne in an exhibition game, the Big Red suffered three straight losses. Capital held the Big Red to four hits in winning 7-0, Oberlin edged the Big Red 11-10 in 12 innings, and Lockbourne won an exhibition game 7-2. Denison then rebounded to win five of its last six games, losing only to Ohio Wesleyan 9-2, and defeating its early season conqueror, Capital, 10-5 in thirteen innings.

Bob Vogt led the hitters with a .395 average, the team as a whole batting over .300.

Fourth Inning

Even though these pages will continue to relate primarily to baseball and softball, I'll use a few lines here to speak more specifically to those of you who are also golfers. Once you determine your eye dominance, if you find you're trying to hit the golf ball from the wrong side, please don't become excessively despondent. I don't profess to know anything about golf as it relates to eye dominance other than my own personal experience.

I could suggest, however, that if you are trying to hit all those golf balls from the wrong side, as I did, that you simply buy a driver for the opposite side. If you sneak in a few good shots with that club and it really works for you, consider making a complete change to hitting from the other side. The purchase of that club won't be wasted anyway. Certainly you get stuck behind a rock or tree now and then. That club could provide an easy way out. A new set of clubs with hitting faces reversed may be a great idea for next year's Christmas present to yourself.

Have you noticed the smooth, effortless, and accurate left-handed swing Phil Michelson possesses? He's right-handed and 80 percent chance he's right-eye dominant too. Phil writes his score card and signs autographs right-handed. He also tosses souvenir balls to his spectators right-handed. He's probably right-eyed.

My continuing aim in this book is to encourage swinging from the correct side, just as I think Phil Michelson does. His stronger power hand is his right hand at the end of the club, providing excellent power advantage. How smooth, accurate, and powerful his left-handed swing.

How could we have been kept in the dark for so many years regarding dominant eyedness as it relates to sports with the two-handed side-on-swing? I think it is just one of those scientific facts that has been unnoticed or ignored as it applies so directly to baseball and softball and the two-handed side-on-swing.

Sometimes we humans just don't pay enough attention to things directly under our noses, things that should be more obvious to us. It is the two-handed side-on-swing that provides the complicating issue.

When I was only four years old, I had an experience that relates directly to ocular dominance or eyedness. Our neighbor across South Defiance Street in Archbold, Ohio, called to me across the street. I was trying to catch grasshoppers in our front yard at the time. Dad said he'd take me fishing after work that day. He said I should catch some grasshoppers for fish bait. Our nice neighbor told me to ask my mom if I could come to their house to have cake and ice cream. Mom heard her request and said, "Sure you can go, just be very careful. Look both ways as you cross the street, just as we practiced last week."

As I was crossing the street only moments later, I thought I had looked both ways. Only eight feet into the street there were horrible sounds of screeching tires and the clatter of metal and car horns as a small truck came to a stop right against my shoulder. My frantic dear mother and other people in homes nearby came quickly to help. Nobody got hurt and the driver of the truck seemed very upset with me. Obviously, I had not turned my head full left as Mom had taught me to do. I am right-eyed. What a lesson for me. To this day, I still turn my head full left, then full right, before crossing a street. This is just another example of the significance of eyedness as it affects our lives.

Mom gave me another lesson on crossing our street after dinner that evening. That took about twenty minutes. Dad and I still had time to go fishing. I think we caught a few small fish, but Dad really seemed to be upset about my street crossing deal that day, so he didn't talk much about fishing.

The very next day my mom took me to our doctor to have my eyes tested. He said my eyes were fine and then said, "Art, you should listen to your mom about crossing streets."

CHAPTER 5

Fifth Inning

During my thirty teaching years in Ohio and in Lake Forest, Illinois, I taught classes in physical science, biology, earth science, general science, and German. For twelve years of this time, I was principal of Lake Forest West Campus High School. During my teaching years, I also coached baseball, basketball, football, and tennis.

Lake Forest High School in Illinois is one of the finest high schools in the United States. This school has a tradition of excellence dating back to 1935 and certainly extending to now in 2018.

I enjoyed every day of my career in high school education. Our talented young people in this great country provide me with great optimism for our future. The spirit of entrepreneurship and exploration are always alive and well in the minds of our youth.

For twenty-four years following my retirement from Lake Forest High School in 1986, I sold real estate in the area. This career change in 1986 provided me with much free time to attend athletic events in the Chicago area. As I watched games in baseball, softball, soccer, football, lacrosse, hockey, tennis, golf, and basketball, I found myself questioning and analyzing the eyedness factors of the various athletes involved in most of the contests. Yes, I enjoyed the games themselves in addition to the eyedness issues that intrigued me.

It was during my first year as a general science teacher at Swanton High School in Ohio that we discussed the subject of ocular dominance during one class period. On the previous day, I had read an interesting article in a science magazine on the topic. I used some of that information to promote the class experimentation and discussion. It was a very lively class that day with students noting very quickly how their one eye can play tricks on them, as they took the test that you have taken.

After class that day, one very bright young student athlete said to me, "No wonder I can't hit a baseball batting right-handed. I wonder if I should try batting left-handed." I encouraged him to try that. He was for sure right-eyed. However, he continued to bat right-handed because his older brother insisted on it. He excelled in basketball and football but was a very average .220 hitter in baseball. He continued to swing the bat from the wrong side of the plate. A little encouragement from that older brother to change his batting side may have been very helpful. But we certainly can't fault an older brother, who probably had no information regarding the eyedness factor that I'm discussing in this book. I did not have the immense confidence in my hypothesis then that I have today either. Each player should at least give his or her correct side a fair try.

A few years ago, our Kleck family gathered at Ruihley Park in Archbold, Ohio, as we had done for many years before. It was our annual family reunion time. There was always plenty of outdoor space to hit Wiffle balls by the many kids at our reunions. My mother, Thelma Kleck, the Cookie Lady, as she was lovingly known in northwest Ohio, was ninety-seven at the time of that reunion.

For years, she had been the favorite of all the kids and adults at our reunions. Often she announced the start of the Wiffle ball hitting contest. In keeping with the tradition, she again announced the start of the Wiffle ball hitting experience with Art pitching and the kids hitting. This happy experience went on for ninety minutes to two hours on this day each year. Some of those wonderful kids knew they could even get started a little early if Mom put pressure on Art to start early.

We always used baseball-sized Wiffle balls and plastic hollow bats so none of the kids would get hurt. I always did the pitching and the kids did the hitting and the fielding. The kids took turns batting during these annual events. Kids from age four to age eighteen participated. Some of the older kids would help the younger kids get started. I threw pitches to each batter until a few pitches were hit fairly. The hitter would then pass the bat to the next kid in line. After his or her turn hitting, that person moved to the outfield and threw the balls back to the pitcher's mound where one active youngster tossed them into the five gallon bucket directly behind the pitcher. It's a lively game. Nobody ever gets hurt. We use lightweight hollow plastic bats and the two kinds of Wiffle balls that I talked about earlier. I try to give the older kids more challenging pitches. They like it that way. Try this game at your next family reunion or neighborhood party. Kids like the game, and it moves along at a lively pace. It is very safe too. Following this activity at our annual family reunions, homemade ice cream is always served.

At this particular reunion a few years ago, I took special note of my nine-year-old nephew, Robbie Bugbee, and my eight-year-old niece, Cassidy Wyse. That day these two kids hit so consistently well, and most of their hits were line drives too. Most of the kids, ranging in age from four to eighteen, would hit four of ten pitches thrown in the strike zone. Robbie and Cassidy hit nearly every pitch I threw them that day. Robbie Bugbee and Cassidy Wyse are both left-eye dominant and swing the bat from the right-hand batter's box. Both throw a ball right-handed and write right-handed. Each is in fact, batting from his and her correct side.

In all the years thereafter, Cassidy and Robbie have continued their spectacular hitting, each from her and his correct side.

With the 2013 school year completed, Cassidy's high school

Cassidy Wyse - 2013

softball team finished with 22 wins and 2 loses. Cassidy had just completed her junior year. She was named first team, All-Ohio Women's Softball team and finished with a batting average of .511. As a third baseman, she finished the year with only one error. Her left-eyedness is also a great asset to her in playing third base as she plays well off the line. I'll explain this later, as I deal with defense and ocular dominance. Cassidy's batting average in fast-pitch softball, her sophomore varsity year was .485. She made second team All-Ohio as a sophomore. *Wow.* I hope you can guess that I am really proud of these kids.

My nephew, Robbie, the very outstanding left-eyed right-handed hitter is continuing his athletic excellence. He's now a high school senior and is a very accomplished lacrosse player. He was also excellent in football, basketball, and baseball. He has decided to give lacrosse his full-time sports attention. He's extremely fast, loves lacrosse, is very well-conditioned, and a prolific lacrosse scorer. Today at the age of eighteen, he is recognized as one of the most outstanding high school lacrosse players in the state of North Carolina. The sport of lacrosse is also highly dependent on eye-hand coordination. The speedy Robbie also thrives on the need for the athleticism and the rough and tumble play lacrosse requires.

Grandma Jan started Robbie on the right track at age three when she tossed nerf balls to Robbie and expected him to hit them back to her. He did exactly that with his little plastic bat. When Robbie tried to bat left-handed, Grandma Jan Kleck again told him to bat right-handed. He became very skilled at doing that. Grandma Jan, you are a truly great early childhood coach.

Our Wiffle ball hitting game at the 2013 June family reunion featured a surprise visit from one of my favorite nephews, Tyler Kleck. Tyler is now thirty-one years old and is now a very successful architect in New York City. When Tyler attended our reunions as a little kid, he was an avid participant in the annual Wiffle ball games. He's a good athlete and while at Napoleon High School in Ohio, he was an excellent varsity player in football, basketball, and baseball.

During the annual Wiffle ball game at the Kleck reunion, Tyler watched the little kids hit and field Wiffle balls for a long time. I knew he was itching to get into the batter's box and hit a few.

When most of the kids had finished the Wiffle ball game and were off eating homemade ice cream, I asked Tyler to pick up a bat and hit. He stood at the plate to bat right-handed. I had tested him earlier in the day and found him to be strongly right-eye dominant. I said to him, "Tyler, I know from the eye test I gave you two hours ago that you are strongly right-eyed. Try batting left-handed just for me." He smiled broadly and said he never once tried batting left-handed, but he'd give it a try. Try it, he did. Tyler hit twelve consecutive hot line drives, all of them while batting left-handed. He smiled and said, "I have never before even swung at a ball left-handed." His performance that day really pleased me, but did not surprise me. He's still an excellent athlete at age thirty-one. He then said as he dropped the bat, "I wish I had tried batting left-handed in high school and college." Tyler is right-eyed and should swing left-handed for greatest success. He said he'd try hitting golf balls left-handed too. I'll check with him on this at our 2018 Kleck reunion.

Many right-handed batters who have great difficulty hitting a right-handed pitcher's curveball or slider go to switch hitting just to survive and to avoid the breakaway pitch. That is a good stopgap measure, but these hitters should take a deep breath and take things one step further. They should do all of their swinging from their newly found correct side. Practice, practice from your correct side. You'll be amazed at how rapidly you will improve your hitting. It is easier to change an old bad habit "wrong side swing" than you may think. Your confidence will build quickly as you see the ball better as you swing from your correct side.

It is important to note here that people experience varying degrees of right-eyedness and left-eyedness. Regardless of the degree of difference, however, it is still smart to let eye dominance only determine each person's correct side swing. It should be noted, however that people who are very strongly right-eyed or strongly left-eyed have most to gain by making a side change.

Stan Musial was strongly right-eyed. He told me that day in 1954 that he simply could not see pitched balls well when he tried batting right-handed. In his twenty-two years with the Cardinals, he obviously saw the ball well batting left-handed. His lifetime average was a splendid .331.

About two months ago, I was out for a walk in our Libertyville neighborhood. Grandpa John McWilliams and his two grandsons were in grandpa's front yard. Grandson Teddy, who is nine, was throwing Wiffle balls to Grandson Daniel, who is twelve. Grandpa John and Grandma Evvie were standing by giving the boys encouragement and some fielding help. Daniel was hitting the ball extremely well left-handed. Nearly every swing produced a line drive. Grandpa John praised Daniel for his excellent left-handed hitting and then encouraged him to bat right-handed also. Daniel resisted this advice from Grandpa John. Then Grandpa John said to me, "Art, don't you think Daniel should also try batting right-handed and perhaps be a switch-hitter?" I answered very honestly and said, "No, I don't think Daniel should be a switch-hitter. I think he's batting from his correct side now. Let's check Daniel's eye dominance." I knew Grandpa John and Grandma Evvie would not be offended at my candid answer. I then explained eyedness to Grandpa and Grandma McWilliams and Grandsons Daniel and Teddy Sennott.

We all did the eye dominance test right there in the front yard. Daniel, the grandson who had been hitting the ball so well left-handed, is strongly right-eyed. Yes, Daniel should absolutely bat left-handed. Grandpa John then said, "It's easy to give the wrong advice to kids if one doesn't know the facts." I quickly explained to them that apparently most people don't realize the significance of right-eyedness and left-eyedness as it pertains to the side-on-swing in baseball and softball. Grandson Daniel then said, "I didn't know about that stuff either, but Grandpa, you know about most things." Grandpa John responded happily, "Daniel, you just continue batting left-handed all the time. I think Art really knows what he's talking about." I then explained to Grandpa John that I'm in process of writing a book on this very subject. I promised Grandpa John McWilliams that I would find a place in my book to relay this experience in their front yard.

Are you beginning to understand why your eye dominance should determine your correct side swing? You'll understand it even better when you personally give it a full effort try. Remember most of us had no good sound scientific information when we first chose our swing side. We chose that side when we were just a little kid or when our parents or grandparents or friends helped us decide which way to swing the bat. How haphazard is that? Let's correct it now if you are swinging from the incorrect side.

Remember when Grandma Jan Kleck realized how very successful Robbie was when swinging right-handed? She insisted that he continue to swing right-handed even when little three-year-old Robbie wanted to try swinging left-handed. Why should she permit him to be less successful than he had been? Grandma Jan is a great early childhood coach. Build on what has proven to be positive. Robbie's well-hit nerf balls of those early years became well-hit baseballs in recent years.

Batters who are right-handed and right-eyed should bat left-handed. These batters should generate maximum power along with an accurate swing. Ted Williams, the great Boston Red Sox player, was exactly this player. Ted Williams had his power hand, right at the knob of the bat. His swing was smooth, powerful, and accurate. His lifetime batting average with the Boston Red Sox was .344. He led the American League in batting six times from 1939 through 1960. He hit 521 home runs and was named player of the decade from 1951–1960. Ted Williams threw the ball right-handed. He was equal-eyed.

Of all professional league players who ever played baseball, it can be argued on pretty safe grounds that Cool Papa Bell of the Negro League was among the very best to ever play baseball. Maybe, on second thought, he and the great Babe Ruth should tie for highest honors. Just my opinion.

Cool Papa Bell always carried a very high batting average .375 to .450. He was a speedy center fielder with great fielding and throwing skills. He moved easily and accurately to any outfield spot to retrieve a ball. Old timers told me he was an absolute joy to watch play this game on offense or defense. He was the very best of switch-hitters with equally high averages from either side of the plate.

I have no way of knowing for sure, but all of his statistics, both offense and defense, suggest that Cool Papa Bell was probably equal-eye dominant. His proven ability to hit equally well from either side of the plate and his uncanny center fielder capabilities to move, right or left or in or out to make all of those very smooth plays; it all suggests equal-eyedness.

If you have by now proved to yourself, through trying the eye dominance test, that you are right-eyed and you are also a right-handed person, please demonstrate to yourself that your right hand is also your power hand. To prove this to yourself, grasp a baseball bat slightly above the knob with your right hand. Pretend you are standing in the left hand batter's box and side-on facing the pitcher with your right eye closest to the pitcher. Now take a left-handed swing with only this right hand grasping the bat. You should be able to take a pretty hard swing at an imaginary pitch from that position. That's your power hand since you are a right-handed person swinging from the correct left-hand batter's box. Note how smooth the swing, even with only one hand on the bat. Now under these conditions when you place the left hand on the bat above the right hand that left hand becomes the guide hand directing the bat with maximum accuracy to hit the ball.

Please keep in mind that the left or guide hand wears the glove when you are in the field on defense. You've trained that left hand to go where the ball is through many years of playing pitch and catch with your friends.

If the batter hits from the newly confirmed correct side, the breakaway pitch should make little difference in each batter's ability to follow and hit the ball. Just hit from the correct side all the time. That's what Joe DiMaggio did. That's what Yogi Berra did. That's what Stan Musial did. None of these great players went to switch-hitting to correct a hitting deficit.

As I mentioned earlier, Stan Musial has always been a favorite baseball player of mine. He was always a St. Louis Cardinal player through his twenty-two seasons in the National League. Stan signed autographs right-handed and threw balls and batted left-handed. These facts suggest great dexterity in both the right and left hands and arms of Stan Musial. Remember the test that day in 1954 that proved that he was right-eyed? His lifetime batting average in the National League was .331. His bronze plaque in the Cooperstown Hall of Fame notes many of his accomplishments including that he won seven National League batting titles. He was also a great gentleman and always the pride of St. Louis.

Ted Williams, the great Boston Red Sox player, interrupted his playing career twice to serve in the United States military service. He served in both World War II and then again during the Korean War that ended in 1953. He served as an air force pilot. Ted Williams was equal-eyed and therefore experienced no blind spots in his vision. This is an ideal situation for an air force pilot.

World War II was an immensely stressful time in our United States history. Our president, Franklin Delano Roosevelt, urged that major league baseball continue through that war period, even though many team owners had volunteered to discontinue play if temporary stoppage could help the war effort. My friends and I were very happy that the sixteen major league teams continued to play. Minor league teams also continued to play. At that time, there were eight teams in the American League and eight teams in the National League. At the end of each baseball season, the winner of the American League would meet the winner of the National League to determine the winner of the World Series in a seven-game playoff series. Television did not exist then for the American public. Radio broadcasts of games, the newspaper sports pages, and sports magazines provided our way of keeping up with our favorite teams and players.

On many of our family trips to and through St. Louis to visit family and friends in St. Louis and Springfield Missouri after 1954 we'd stop at *Musial and Biggies*, a great St. Louis restaurant. We saw Stan Musial there on several occasions after 1954. He always checked on my progress regarding the book. I kept telling him I just hadn't found the time but would do it someday. He would say to me, "I'm still checking my friends' eyedness." He was especially happy to report to me that Ted Williams was equal-eyed. Stan Musial had tested him at a Baseball All-Star Game. Since Ted Williams was a right-handed person, he always had his power hand at the knob of the bat when hitting the ball. This is the ideal situation for maximum hitting power when batting left-handed. He also said he thought Joe DiMaggio must be equal-eyed too since he had played center field so flawlessly. He did not test DiMaggio, however. He then said, "If Joe DiMaggio is not equal-eyed, he is for sure left-eyed. He's always been a great right-handed hitter."

Sixth Inning

Larger numbers of batters in the future will bat from the left-hand batter's box as players learn and better understand the scientific advantages of batting from the correct side of the plate. The shorter distance to first base from the left-hand batter's box will also make for more runners reaching first base safely.

Batting from the correct side also adds a great safety factor to the game. When I was a kid playing baseball and softball, no batting helmets were worn by batters. Some of my friends did not play baseball because they were afraid to stand in the batter's box when the pitcher delivered the ball. I predict that in the future many more young men and young women will play baseball and softball. It's much easier to see the ball accurately when batting from the correct side.

When I was a kid in the 1930s and 1940s, most of us got little or no official coaching in baseball or softball until our high school days. Kids often organized their own teams and games and moms and dads or the kids themselves did the coaching and umpiring. A player would typically swing the bat from the side that seemed most comfortable. Usually right-handed kids batted right-handed and left-handed kids batted left-handed. Even today, it is true that most right-handed kids bat right-handed and most left-handed kids bat left-handed.

Let's try to get this corrected beginning now. Let eye dominance assist us in our decisions. Under these circumstances, most right-handed kids will bat left-handed and most left-handed kids will bat right-handed. Striking out is no fun for anyone. Hitting the ball solidly is fun for everyone.

Are you really ready to take some risks and make some important changes if your eye dominance test tells you that you've been batting from the incorrect side? My advice is this. At the very least, give the correct side a solid try. You'll surprise yourself with the great results.

The ever existing spirit of competition among athletes for team starting positions will help sort it all out. Athletes who take the risks to do it correctly will ultimately make the team's starting lineup.

Certainly, Babe Ruth dominated the great sport of baseball during his twenty-two years of major league play. No strength enhancing drugs, just a great athlete performing at a high level. He endeared the American public to him and his accomplishments. Through his time in the baseball spotlight, America realistically called baseball "the great American pastime." "The Babe" was officially at bat 8,399 times and collected 2,873 hits. His lifetime batting average, playing initially for the Boston Red Sox and then for the New York Yankees was .342.

He punctuated these many hits with seven hundred fourteen homers, some of them very dramatic. Even though he played his last Yankee major league game about eighty years ago, he still epitomizes the best of the baseball athlete.

He began his major league career as a very dominant left-handed pitcher with the Boston Red Sox. As a pitcher he is in the record books with ninety-four major league wins and only forty-six losses. His earned run average as a pitcher was a neat 2.28 ERA. His bronze plaque in the Baseball Hall of Fame notes the details.

Ultimately, it was Babe Ruth's consistent and powerful hitting, however, that kept him in the lineup every day. His excellent fielding abilities and his strong and accurate throwing skills made him the complete player. He also wanted to play every day and pitchers cannot pitch every day. The pitcher's arm requires rest time between games.

The Boston Red Sox sold Babe to the New York Yankees in 1919. Many fine books have been written about Babe Ruth. I think he richly deserved every accolade sent his way. I am firmly convinced that Babe Ruth was right-eyed. I'll convey to you a conversation I had with Mr. Robert Worst of Dayton, Ohio, that solidly confirms this.

I entered Denison University in Granville, Ohio, in September of 1949. I pledged the Kappa Sigma Fraternity during the second week of school. My big brother in Kappa Sigma was Bob Worst, a junior. A big brother was assigned to each new pledge to assist each new kid in adjusting to the new scholastic and social environment and to prod the young student in his academic endeavors. Bob Worst was a wonderful and very thoughtful big brother.

On one occasion, he invited me to his home in Dayton, Ohio. Bob's parents were very cordial people, and I enjoyed the weekend in Dayton immensely. My big brother informed his dad, Bob Worst, Sr., that I was a baseball player, a pitcher. Bob Worst, Sr., and I got into a lengthy conversation about Major League Baseball.

Mr. Worst worked for a radio station in Dayton, Ohio. I had the very pleasant experience of listening to him on the radio that weekend. During that weekend, he told me that he had once interviewed the great Babe Ruth and found him to be very friendly and thoughtful and eager to share some of his experiences. Mr. Worst told me that Babe Ruth was just as talented on defense as he was as a hitter. He observed that he was an excellent defensive outfielder. He said, "Frankly, Babe Ruth did everything well in baseball, including running the bases and even stealing bases now and then." He commented that Babe Ruth had an excellent throwing arm and that he had the uncanny ability to always throw to the right spot or base after retrieving a ball in the outfield. During his interview with Babe Ruth, Mr. Worst asked him if he had ever tried batting right-handed. Babe Ruth's answer was, "I tried that a few times, but I just couldn't see the ball very well, so I've always batted left-handed." He must have been right-eyed.

I went to a Chicago area large sports equipment store a few weeks ago, one that sells a very high volume of golf equipment. I observed that most of the golf clubs for sale were for right-handed players. I asked the salesman which clubs he would recommend for me. His first question was "Are you right-handed or left-handed?" I told him that I was right-handed, but that I am also right-eyed. He said, "That should make no difference." Then he said, "Right-handers should always use right-handed clubs." Then he looked at me very strangely and asked me if I had ever played golf. I told him that I had played forty-five years ago. I told him I had just not been good at it. "Hitting the ball was a real challenge to me," I told him. He quickly replied, "You probably didn't keep your head down when you attempted to hit the ball." My response, "I heard that several times each day I played. I just couldn't do that, I guess." I then asked him if he thought it would be better for me to get left-handed clubs and just play golf left-handed. He said he could not recommend that under any circumstances. Then he said, "I just wouldn't feel right about selling you left-handed clubs since you are right-handed." Just then his cell phone rang, he answered it and moved away from me. I am really not sure, but I think that by this time he was guessing that this old man, I am eighty-eight, needed more help than he could provide. I left the store smiling. He waved from afar as I thanked him for his help. I've gone back to that same store to ask more questions about golf clubs and baseball bats. When the same young man saw me approaching the last time I was in the store, he turned his back and answered his cell phone. Perhaps he was just calling for help.

I've gone to several other sports equipment stores in the Chicago area, big stores with massive sports equipment inventories. None of the salespeople, including store managers, seem to know anything about eyedness. One store manager simply said, "It sounds very confusing, I'd turn customers away if I even mentioned it."

Yes, I can easily imagine how a salesperson could easily turn a potential buyer away when a customer asks to look at right-handed golf clubs and the sales person quickly asks, "What is your eyedness or ocular dominance?" The new customer who has probably played poorly for twenty years simply wants a new set of more up-to-date and fancier clubs. Anything to improve his game. He does not want to be confused by such questioning. He just wants a new set of clubs, some of those advertised on television that will help him hit the ball better. After hitting right-handed for all those years, why would he change hitting sides? How confusing. You've got it right, the sales-person will not confuse his potential golf club buyer, with some scientific questioning. He'll just sell the frustrated golfer a fancier set of clubs and tell him, "Good luck and keep your head down."

Will you golfers please take me seriously as I suggest that you try the other side if the eye test tells you that you are swinging from the incorrect side? My suggestion is this. At least give the correct side a try. Who knows? Maybe you are missing out on lots of golfing fun and lower scores too. If the left-handed driver pleases you, maybe you should ask for a set of left-handed clubs for Christmas.

Perhaps most or all of the very best golfers on the pro circuit are already swinging from the correct side. Maybe those players can't even begin to understand the frustrations felt by those of us who have tried to hit those little white balls from the wrong side. The profitable business of golf lessons would likely decline sharply if all beginning golfers hit from the correct side. Hitting from the correct side could only improve the overall quality of golf.

I explained earlier, however, that I claim no real knowledge of the sport of golf. I was a completely inept golfer. I toss in these comments only because golf uses the side-on-swing, and for myself, I have learned recently that I can actually hit a golf ball consistently well with my new left-handed driver. That is why I'm suggesting to those of you who are not very good golfers, but like the game, that you at least borrow or purchase a driver with the opposite face from your other clubs and give it a try. Please do this only if you are still hitting from the incorrect side.

CHAPTER 7

Seventh Inning

Now back to baseball and fast-pitch softball. If a player begins his or her hitting days from the correct side of the plate, with reasonable practice, improvement can be constant. On the other hand, if a player sees some reason to try switch-hitting, that player has lost some confidence and is personally feeling a handicap that perhaps could be corrected by hitting from the correct side. I contend that once a player hits successfully from the correct side, the player usually won't want to go back to the old hitting side. Hitting is much more comfortable from the correct side.

Our 1953 Denison University baseball team shared the conference championship with Ohio Wesleyan. Our leading hitter on this team was Bob Vogt, a truly great athlete. His 1953 season batting average was .395. By the way, Bob was a right-handed batter and is for sure left-eye dominant. He is also a member of the Denison Athletic Hall of Fame. I tested Bob Vogt's left-eyedness after his eighty-first birthday during a Denison University reunion. Bob also still holds the Denison football scoring record he set during the Denison 1953 football season. He was a very fast halfback and a good pass catcher. He scored 119 points that season. His record still stands. Bob was also Denison's leading punter in 1952. He averaged forty yards per punt and was a right-footed punter. His left-eye dominance was also a very positive factor here as his left eye never lost sight of the ball as the ball and his right foot met to achieve the best punt possible.

Bob Vogt was not a power hitter in baseball or softball, but he was an immensely high average hitter in both sports. His power hand was not at the knob of the bat as is the case with most power hitters I've studied.

Even at the age of eighty-five, Bob Vogt is still an excellent golfer. He still shoots in the middle eighties. He is hitting from his correct right-handed side now and has always hit from his correct side. None of his playing or practice time has been wasted.

I mentioned earlier that Bob was an excellent pass receiver out of the backfield, especially when he was moving at an angle from right sideline toward left sideline. His left-eyedness was a great asset to him then also as he looked back to the quarterback.

Midway through our 1953 Denison baseball season, I asked my coach, Keith Piper, if I could bat left-handed for the balance of the season. We faced mostly right-handed pitchers and I just couldn't hit those curveballs. I was just waving at most of them. Keith said, "Just do it if you think you can get a few hits for us batting left-handed. I started batting left-handed that day and my hitting improved." Then he cautioned, "Don't get hit on the right elbow."

Herein lies the reason most coaches, even to this day, don't want right-handed pitchers to bat left-handed. Pitchers with injured elbows can't pitch effectively. My high school coach, Don Hornish, did not want me to try batting left-handed for that same reason. Mr. Hornish was an excellent baseball coach. All of my coaches in both high school and college were great people and excellent coaches.

Since everyone can see and follow the ball much better when batting from his or her correct side, it should be quite evident that fewer injuries would be caused by pitched balls when batters are batting from the correct side. All pitches are easier to see more accurately when the dominant eye, the truth-telling eye, is in charge and nearest the pitcher.

Another excellent athlete on our Denison 1953 baseball team was Don Alt. Don was our 175 pound, right-handed right-eyed shortstop. Don was a .340 power hitter with good speed, strong right arm, and very accurate throw to first base or home plate. Yes, he batted left-handed just as all right-eyed players should bat. His left-handed swing was smooth and accurate and powerful. Don and I were co-captains of that 1953 championship team. All players on this team and Coach Keith Piper deserve full credit for our success. Good people and good athletes. Don Alt is for sure right-eyed. I personally tested him again after his eighty-third birthday. He also received Little All-American football honors following the 1952 football season at Denison. Add to this that Don began playing competitive racquetball in 1972 at age forty-one.

For the fifteen years ending in 2007 the National Racquetball Association (USAR) accumulated points earned by all players in the United States. Don Alt ranked sixth among the top five hundred players in gold points earned over those fifteen years in the United States. Racquetball is a sport that also requires excellent eye-hand coordination for maximum success. Don Alt is also a charter member of the National Masters' Racquetball Hall of Fame established in 1994. Both Bob Vogt and Don Alt are members of the Denison University Athletic Hall of Fame.

We had a feisty and very talented catcher on our 1953 baseball team. His name is Carl Jochens, a Chicago boy. He was a major reason I was a successful college pitcher. I could throw the off the plate outside curveball in the dirt anytime and Carl could catch it. Even though Carl weighed only 165 pounds and was five feet eight he could block the plate and catch and throw with the very best collegiate catchers. He kept us laughing with his great sense of humor and was the key player of a good defensive team. Thanks, Carl.

While observing various teams carefully during my lifetime, I have observed that most successful baseball teams at all levels of competition rely on an excellent catcher as the core and captain of their defense. The New York Yankee's Yogi Berra in the 1940s and 1950s, and the Cincinnati Reds' Johnny Bench in the 1960s and 1970s are examples of this at the Major League level. These players were good on both defense and offense and both were highly regarded by their teammates as defensive "take charge" players. Both were excellent leaders.

The best position for the team leader on any baseball or softball team is the catcher's position. The catcher has the best view of the total field and the smart catcher should quickly learn the strengths and weaknesses of opposing hitters. The catchers noted here were immensely helpful to their pitchers and to all defensive players on their teams.

Having lived in the Chicago area for fifty-six years, I've become one of those eternal optimists regarding the Chicago Cubs. With the Cubs' new and more aggressive ownership and management leading the way, I am confident that the Cubs will play in another World Series within two years. I also predict that the well managed Chicago White Sox will play in the World Series within two years.

CHAPTER 8

Eighth Inning

Let's talk about another very important aspect of baseball and softball—fielding your position. Your improved knowledge of right-eyedness and left-usedness will help you in your fielding techniques also.

A center fielder is usually assigned that position by coaches and managers because that player is the fastest player on the team and seems equally competent in going right or left or back or in for the fly ball or hit.

Excellent throwing ability, both accuracy and distance throws, are another requirement. The center fielder is placed varying distances behind second base and about in line with second base and home plate. The center fielder should really be the captain of the outfield, and if possible, know the tendencies of the opponent hitters. Good coaches often convey information concerning the opponent hitters to the center fielder captain so he or she can better direct or assist the right and left fielders in their combined fielding responsibilities.

Joe DiMaggio of the New York Yankees was the premier center fielder in the major leagues in my boyhood days. He was extremely fast and could, with nearly flawless movement, go back, run in, or move right or left in fielding his position. I attended one New York Yankee game at Briggs Stadium in Detroit primarily to watch Joe DiMaggio play. He was a defensive genius and a great hitter.

Baseball experts of past and present consider him one of the very best "go get 'em" outfielders of all time. His Hall of Fame commendations in Cooperstown are the best. He always carried a high batting average and was a solid line drive hitter, even his home runs.

He batted right-handed always. He hit safely in fifty-six consecutive Major League games, still a record today. His crisp right-handed throwing ability was flawless. His poise in moving easily any direction from his center field position to make very smooth plays even suggests that he may have been equal-eye dominant. He always gave both right and left fielders lots of help in fielding their positions. By the way, Joe never saw any reason to switch-hit. He hit right and left-handed pitchers equally well, always from the right-hand batter's box.

Many of you have probably known players who make better and more excellent and smoother plays running one way, but not the reverse. I'll call this their correct side. If the defensive player is right-eyed he or she will usually make smoother and better plays while running left. Remember, in these cases the fielder's dominant eye is in direct line with the hitter and the ball as the right-eyed fielder runs left toward the right field foul line and the left-eyed fielder runs right toward the left field foul line. If the coach or manager knows the dominant evenness of each of his players he can better place them in advantageous fielding positions for each opponent hitter. Players and coaches can quickly see the advantages to be gained from knowing and sharing this information.

Here is a good example: A third baseman who is right-eyed should play very close to the third base foul line. Chances are good that this player can move easily and accurately toward the shortstop or left to field a ball. The player's dominant eye will be facing the batter as he or she moves left. By playing close to the third base line this player also places himself or herself in an excellent position to field the "hot smash" down the third base line to avoid the potential double.

In my view, it is very important for coaches to know and understand the eye dominance of each of their defenders, thereby assisting these players appropriately for each opposing hitter.

The catcher is often the defensive captain and can be of great help here. In order to do the job effectively, the catcher must know the eyedness or eye dominance of each teammate. Remember, the right-eyed outfielder will move smoothly and accurately toward the right field line and the left-eyed outfielder will move smoothly and accurately toward the left field line. Let's call this applied eye science for the defense.

A few years ago, I stopped by a summer baseball practice session in Libertyville, Illinois. I watched as the players went through various fielding drills. One of the coaches at one point was hitting fungos, mostly fly balls, to his players as they were moving on a run, sometimes slowly and sometimes fast, from about seventy-five feet inside the left field foul line toward the right field foul line to catch or catch up to a ball near center field. Most of the nineteen players handled this drill rather easily. The boys displayed excellent fielding and throwing skills. Only two of those players seemed to have considerable difficulty with this drill. The two that had problems were probably left-eye dominant.

I understood as I watched why seventeen of the players handled this drill with ease. All except two of the nineteen players in the drill were right-handed and since about 80 to 85 percent of right-handers are right-eyed most of the players were running their correct direction to see the ball accurately.

Right-eyed players field balls most easily when looking back to the batter with the right eye nearest the batter as they run left. Then the coach continued the same drill, but this time, starting players from about seventy-five feet from the right field foul line. The coach again hit fungos, mostly fly balls, to his players as they ran from the right field foul line toward center field. Many of the nineteen players experienced great difficulty in doing this. In fact, some who had been very effective moving from the left field foul line toward center field were most at a loss in handling this drill, now running from right field foul line toward center field. I observed that neither the players nor the coach understood why this problem existed. I knew the answer, but I did not inject myself into the situation. Here was the challenge: As all of these nineteen players were now running toward the left field line, please keep in mind that most of them were probably right-eyed. Their dominant eye was now away from the batter as they ran from the right field foul line toward center field. Following the ball accurately should be more difficult for the right-eyed players, that is, for most of them. The two players who had great difficulty with the previous drill were excellent on this reverse drill.

The dominant eyes of probably seventeen of these players were now away from the batter as they headed toward center field. Following the ball accurately should be much more difficult for these right-eyed players. Please remember that there were only two left-handed players in this group of nineteen. Also remember that 80 to 85 percent of right-handed people are also right-eyed. No wonder this group of athletes experienced a major challenge when running in a line from right field foul line toward center.

Should I have talked with the coach and his nineteen players right then? Absolutely not. That coach seemed to have excellent rapport with his players. It would have been very rude and thoughtless of me to intervene. I did, however, try to reach the coach that evening via phone to talk with him about ocular dominance. I failed to reach him then or in three follow-up calls. I'll try him again another day.

What could I have done better as coach of those nineteen boys, knowing what I know about the importance of ocular dominance as it affects the players' fielding skills? First, I would have informed my team members earlier, as I have informed you in this book. I'd try to make sure that each of my players is well informed on the subject of ocular dominance or eyedness. Each of my players would have taken the eye dominance test and, for sure, know his or her own eyedness. The smarter players among the nineteen would begin to coach themselves as they play defense and as they take their place in the correct batter's box. An excellent athlete attempts to improve his or her skills constantly. Good team members also help each other improve. Approaching the ball from a greater angle and then circling in some toward the batted ball is a method that works well for some outfielders. At any rate, it should all begin with an improved understanding of how each player's improved knowledge of eyedness affects what each player sees comfortably. The motion of running also complicates sight concentration on the ball.

Remember that a right-eyed third baseman playing close to the foul line should be able to move smoothly and accurately toward the shortstop position to field a grounder toward the shortstop. Since the shortstop often plays deep in the hole to cut off drives toward second base the right-eyed third baseman actually expands the manager's defensive strength up the middle of the diamond. It is very important for managers and coaches to have this information.

I mentioned earlier in the book that during my freshman and sophomore years at Archbold High School I played center field some of the time. I clearly remember having difficulty following the ball accurately while running across the outfield toward the left field line, yet I had no difficulty following and fielding the ball smoothly moving in the opposite direction, that is from left field foul line toward right field foul line. I now understand this completely. I am right-eye dominant.

The really great professional center fielders of the past, like Joe DiMaggio of the American League, Cool Papa Bell of the Negro League and Mickey Mantle of the American League were probably equal-eye dominant. Those players could move very accurately and quickly in any direction to retrieve a hit or fly ball. Perhaps center fielders who achieved great success and were not equal-eyed worked very hard and practiced diligently and intelligently to place themselves in a proper location for each hitter they faced. Meticulous scouting reports would be extremely valuable to them in achieving fielding excellence.

Good coaches and managers of the future should have a greater interest and purpose in knowing the ocular dominance of each team member. This knowledge would help each place his or her players properly for the team's most effective defense.

Now to summarize and keep it simple: If a batter is right-eyed he or she should bat left-handed. If a fielder is right-eyed that fielder will field balls best while moving left. (Bat left, move left.) If the batter is left-eyed, that batter should bat right-handed. If the fielder is left-eyed that fielder will field balls best when the fielder is moving right. (Bat right, move right). Once you have determined your personal eyedness, it may prove very interesting to you to test your own fielding skills. This would further convince you that I am correct.

CHAPTER 9

Ninth Inning

Now let's talk about bunting. The art of bunting seems to me to be nearly a lost art. Excellent coaches and managers should insist that all players on their teams appropriately handle the responsibility of bunting if the coach calls for a bunt. It is very disheartening to me to watch a major league player, unable to lay down a good bunt whenever called upon to do it. This could easily be a key play of the ball game. Every good player should be a good bunter and welcome the opportunity to do it with perfection. There is absolutely no excuse for not becoming an accomplished bunter in the major leagues and, for that matter, even in less prestigious league situations. Keep in mind please, that bunting should be done from each player's correct side of the plate.

Most pitchers are right-handed and therefore probably 80 to 85 percent of them are also right-eyed. Each player, however, should be individually tested to determine each player's ocular dominance. All players, including pitchers, should bat from the correct side of the plate. I would urge that major league managers, in the National League especially, begin immediately training all of their right-handed pitchers to bunt left-handed, if they are in fact right-eyed. In the American League pitchers seldom bat, due to the designated hitter provision, but who knows, there could be hitting stars among them.

Look at it this way. Since early childhood, most of us played "pitch and catch" with a friend or parent or sibling. We learned to catch the ball with a glove on the nonthrowing hand. For most of us, the left hand was the catching hand. Now transfer this knowledge and experience to the bunting situation. If we are right-eyed, we should bunt left-handed. In most cases our dominant hand, the right hand, will now be at the knob of the bat and our catching hand will be up toward the trademark of the bat. Now when the pitch is delivered, "catch" the ball on the bat with your normal catching hand. This is your guide hand on the bat when bunting. It should really be true that players who can catch a ball with a glove should be able to bunt a ball with a bat. You simply "catch" the ball on the bat instead of with a glove. This applies mostly, of course, when the catching hand is not at the knob of the bat, but rather closest to the middle of the bat.

Since the right-eyed, right-handed player could be the bunter in this case and bunting from the left side, the bunter will be two steps closer to first base and may find it possible to beat out many bunts. Keep in mind that one sees the ball more clearly from the correct side and can therefore place the bunt more accurately. How many times have you watched a right-handed pitcher bunting right-handed to sacrifice a runner along and the bunter misses the ball, thereby striking out and the catcher throws to second base catching the runner for a double play? I've seen that happen far too often in major league games. It's called "strike 'em out, throw 'em out."

Our leading hitter at Denison University, when we won the conference championship in 1953, was Bob Vogt, as I noted earlier. He had a .395 batting average and was also a great "clutch hitter." I don't recall a single time when Bob Vogt was called upon to bunt during that season. I will remind you that he was a right-handed batter who is left-eyed and therefore batted from his correct side. His glove hand was at the knob of the bat. Probably he would not have been a great bunter. Most good coaches and managers will eagerly let an excellent hitter like Bob Vogt "swing away" in all situations. They are the players that coaches and teams rely on to produce the runs batted in and keep the rally going.

Years of practice catching a ball in a glove and thousands of repetitions pay off. That catching hand becomes very well trained through time. Now apply all that catching practice and knowledge to the simple act of bunting from the correct side. Just catch the ball on the bat. It works.

I knew and pitched against a right-handed swinger during my playing days who always bunted left-handed when a sacrifice was in order. Also he would sometimes bunt left-handed in search of a hit. He was an excellent right-handed pitcher and very fast on the base paths. Even though everyone in the park knew he would be bunting when he batted left-handed, he collected many career hits doing that. He was just an average to poor hitter when batting right-handed. He probably would have been an excellent hitter if he had batted left-handed all of the time. I saw him again when he was about fifty years old. When I asked him why he hadn't batted left-handed all the time while playing for his high school team, he told me that his coach would not allow him to do it because "he may sustain a right elbow injury." I noted earlier that during my high school and collegiate playing days, most coaches would not permit right-handed pitchers to bat left-handed. Coaches were concerned that the right elbow would be very easily injured if hit by the baseball. In those days, Tommy John's surgery did not exist to repair elbows. These same coaches did not know that these same right-handed pitchers could have seen pitches much more easily batting from their correct side. All players should bat from their correct side. See the pitch better and avoid getting hit; see the pitch better and get a hit. *What you see is what you hit.* If you swing at what you think you see from the incorrect batter's box, that will most often not be the ball. You haven't let your "truth telling eye" inform you. Please let your "truth telling eye" the dominant one, cooperate with your brain to help you. The other eye gives your brain incorrect information. That eye helps you strike out.

Many good left-handed batters, batting from their correct side, foul off lots of pitches to the third base side. I have observed that these left-handed batters are among the better batters I've seen. They are able to put the bat on the ball late and remain at the plate for another better pitch to hit fairly and squarely.

If most of our batters in baseball and softball became left-handed hitters, as I think will happen, then special safety considerations will have to be made for the fans on the third base side of the stands. This would be the case in all baseball parks. Higher and more protective screens will be necessary. Just imagine how much more this will be needed as the number of left-handed batters increases substantially with more players swinging from the correct side.

Tomorrow's pitchers will be forced to field their positions more effectively than they do today. Why? With more correct-side batters seeing the ball more clearly, batters will hit more hard grounders and line drives right up the middle. Protective head gear may even become the order of the day for pitchers. The pitcher will really be on the firing line facing both right and left-handed swingers batting from the correct side with a more precise view of each pitch. Changes are coming.

I predict that even most of today's switch-hitters will elect to swing from their correct side all of the time. They'll spend their entire batting practice time on their correct side. More practice from the correct side will certainly improve the results. Both ball speed and other ball movement can be more accurately determined from each hitter's correct side.

The new larger number of left-handed hitters will also make good use of the two step advantage in reaching first base safely, whether bunting or hitting away.

The number of slowly hit ground balls should be greatly reduced because of more correct side accurate swings. The number of intentional slow roller bunts should be increased with the hitters' improved abilities to follow all pitchers more meticulously, thereby, making precisely the intended contact with the ball while bunting.

I predict that those players who elect to continue hitting from the wrong side of the plate will be unable to compete with players who take the time and effort to make the smart change. There will be some few players, less than one percent, who have both eyes dominant. They should be able to choose their preferred side.

CHAPTER 10

Tenth Inning

Be inventive and entrepreneurial. Use some of these ideas for your own personal profit. Let your imagination help you. There is much information in these pages that should stir the thinking of many of you readers. Why don't you be one of those ambitious entrepreneurs? Let your clear thinking and ambition earn you a psychological or monetary profit.

Child safety training at the crosswalk presents some very happy possibilities. Children need to know that they can add tremendously to their own safety just by turning head and body far to the left then far to the right to see accurately and clearly. The child should not just be told to look left and right. This should be demonstrated by an adult turning head and body both left and right followed by an explanation to the child that each one of us has one eye that gives him or her more truthful information than the other. Assure the child that this is perfectly normal. Therefore, the child should keep both eyes wide open and continue to look both ways when crossing a street. Kids like to have "why questions" answered even when they don't ask.

Someday when you are watching a football game and you observe the potential pass receiver move from right sideline toward left sideline attempting to catch a pass thrown by the quarterback, if the potential receiver fumbles the ball or perhaps doesn't even touch the football that was within his reach, you might want to guess that the potential receiver is right-eye dominant. His left eye closest to the quarterback did not give him reliable information.

Someday when you have the task of hanging a few large pictures after the painters have painted a few rooms in your home, please step to the correct side of each picture and the task is easy. If you are right-eyed, step to the left as your face each picture. If you are left-eyed, step to the right side as you face the picture. Your view of the nail or hook on the wall will then be at its best.

When you are driving an automobile, know which is your reliable, truth-telling eye. Know which eye plays tricks on you.

When a right-handed quarterback drops back to pass and he gets "blindsided" by a pass rusher coming in on his left, know that the left tackle probably missed his blocking assignment and that the quarterback is probably right-eyed if he is right-handed.

Most assembly lines in manufacturing plants move from left to right. It would really make more sense if more of them moved from right to left, thereby placing the greater percentage of right-eyed workers at greater comfort and efficiency positions. Please remember, a much larger percentage of workers in any manufacturing plant are right-eyed just as most are right-handed.

Managers of manufacturing plants could provide assembly lines moving both directions and give workers a comfort and efficiency choice. If all workers are aware of their individual eyedness through appropriate testing, plant efficiency and safety could be enhanced by simply assigning workers to the appropriate assembly lines. Worker effectiveness, comfort, productivity, and safety could be thereby improved.

Safety screens installed on the front edge of spectator seating down the first and third base lines between home plate and fifty feet beyond both first and third base should be mandatory in all major league parks. Broken bats and hard hit foul balls have become great hazards to the fans. Many of the broken bat situations result from players holding bats incorrectly. The trademark should always face the batter. Carelessness by batters began several years ago when aluminum bats were introduced at Little League, high school, and college levels. As a result, players have developed bad habits. I've watched many major league baseball games via television during the 2010,

2011, 2013, 2014, and 2015, 2016 and 2017 seasons. I counted twelve times during one game where bats were held incorrectly. This should never happen. Since some players are not holding the bat correctly management should be forced to provide some added safety for fans. Wooden bats are designed to not break only if held correctly with the trademark facing the batter. Players who hit a ball with the bat held incorrectly provide a hazard to both fans and other players on the field. My suggestion is this: the umpire should simply call the player out who holds the bat incorrectly. Cameras could verify. The rules committee at the major league level could make this happen.

Automotive and highway safety have been a great concern of mine for many years. Our human eyedness plays a very large role in all of this. Perhaps the British got it right when they decided to drive on the left side of the road with cars passing on the right. Eighty to eighty-five percent of all drivers are right-eyed. I've driven several hundred miles in England and found it to be very easy and frankly quite relaxing. The highway accident rate per miles driven is many percentage points below our United States accident rate. Their feeder roads or entrance roads to major highways are on the left also. Here in the United States approximately 80 to 85 percent of drivers enter our high speed highways with the "truth-telling eye" on the wrong side and attempt to accurately observe the fast-moving traffic on the left. No wonder our United States accident rates are very high. Our "truth-telling eye" is on the incorrect side to provide maximum vision of all those fast-moving vehicles on our left as we enter the major roadways.

I know that our human eyedness is a major factor here. Then I ask what can our United States safety planners, highway engineers, and automotive companies and engineers do to vastly improve our United States auto and highway safety? Human eyedness should be given great consideration. Perhaps a thorough study of the eyedness of our driving population could be given great consideration.

I am confident that the great entrepreneurs, scientists, and leaders among you will insist on better results. New information or old information discovered anew can easily provide an impetus for improvement. Let's do it.

Every driver in the United States is required to take a visual test. Every driver could be informed via this test. Ninety-five percent of humans will have a "blind spot" on the opposite side from that dominate eye. Could such research also show that the 15 to 20 percent of left-eyed drivers have more accident free driving records than the 80 to 85 percent of right-eyed drivers in the United States?

In the years ahead, entrepreneurs, scientists, engineers, and just ordinary people will hopefully use and expand on some of the ideas and observations I've presented here. Child safety, automotive and highway safety, assembly line safety and efficiency, power tool design and safety, baseball stadium safety, heavy equipment design and safety, construction site safety, agricultural equipment design and safety, wood shop equipment design and safety. These are just a few examples of areas that could benefit from proper application of some of the ideas and scientific principles included here. Let your imagination and spirit of entrepreneurship lead you to more. A massive safety study by some of our very best highway engineers and safety experts could find some correct and helpful answers quite easily.

My lovely wife Barbara is left-eyed and is a very excellent and safe driver. She and I have had many helpful conversations regarding eyedness and driving. She is a far better driver than I am in high density traffic and actually in all driving situations.

There is a vast amount of scientific research that needs to be done on the subject of eye dominance and how it affects us in our daily lives. Why don't you do some of it? Don't worry about who gets the credit for accomplishing many steps forward. Harry Truman, our thirty-third president once said, "It's amazing what you can accomplish if you do not care who gets the credit." Let's get on with it.

CHAPTER 11

Eleventh Inning

My conclusions, after my long time experience in playing baseball, softball, basketball, football, and tennis plus coaching many players in these sports leaves me convinced that each athlete's eyedness or eye dominance plays a major role in each athlete's success. The side-on-swing in baseball and softball makes these sports especially influenced by each player's eye dominance or eyedness.

I've been an avid major league baseball fan my entire life. I'd really like to emphasize that these games could be played to their greatest excellence if both players and coaches applied the simple principles I've outlined. Eyedness should be the only issue in determining the correct side swing for each player. The very best hitters of all time have demonstrated a great variety of hitting positions or hitting stances. What is really important is that each player determine his or her correct side swing, then find a comfortable hitting stance, then practice, practice, practice from the correct side.

On the days of the Wiffle ball hitting experiences with nephew Robbie and niece Cassidy and nephew Tanner and all of the other wonderful kids present for our Kleck family reunions; it was then I decided, for sure, that I must convey my observations and conclusions on this subject.

Thank you Robbie, Cassidy, Tanner, Tyler, Sherri, Douglas, David, Tim, Suzie, Penny, Kelly, Mark, Chris, Lance, Oliver, Brady, Jamie, Cody, Lily, Amy, Dan, Courtney, Bridgett, Leslie, Jennifer, Jake, Holly, Matt, Jacki, Jocko, Carla, Becky, Kim, and additional cousins and friends who just dropped in. You are the greatest. You people individually and as a group inspired me to write this book. You provided that final push.

My talented Archbold High School physics teacher and coach, Mervin Farber, planted the idea during that 1948 physics class. The idea and all of the pieces of the puzzle seemed to grow and make constant sense through my various lifetime experiences and observations.

Yes, it should be eyedness or ocular dominance only that determines the side from which each baseball and fast-pitch softball player swings the bat. The batter will see the ball more accurately from the correct side. With the dominant eye positioned closest to the pitcher, the hitter gets the most truthful picture. You can't wear any kind of prescription glasses that alters this. Think back to the experiment to determine your eyedness. Also remember how well Cassidy and Robbie hit the Wiffle balls. Both Cassidy and Robbie are left-eyed and both bat right-handed. It's that side-on-swing in baseball and softball along with the fact that the ball is being thrown toward the batter at varying speeds and movements as well. The batter is forced to make hitting or nonhitting decisions in a very short space of time.

Most of you will recall that the fabulous basketball player, Michael Jordan, first retired from the Chicago Bulls basketball team on October 6, 1993, after having played a key role in three national championships with the Chicago Bulls. He then joined the Chicago White Sox baseball team. White Sox fans' hopes ran high that this splendid athlete and marvelous competitor could also become a dominant athlete on the baseball field. That did not happen.

I think that if Michael Jordan had switched to batting left-handed instead of right-handed, he could have become a star left-handed hitter and an overall star baseball player. He was and still is an incredibly gifted and committed athlete with head, hands, heart, total self, and maximum energy in full focus when competing. One big problem for Michael, he batted right-handed, most likely his incorrect side. Michael is right-handed and therefore 80 to 85 percent chance he is right-eyed and therefore, should have batted left-handed.

We Chicago Bulls' basketball fans are very happy that Michael Jordan elected to come back to the Chicago Bulls and help win three more national championships, surrounded by an outstanding cast of teammates and great coaches.

Talented athletes like Michael Jordan can quite easily make the transition to correct-side hitting. I think he could have made that batting side change easily. When he played basketball for the Chicago Bulls, he was "the best" in every category. Thanks, Michael, for all the genuine enjoyment you provided for your millions of fans. You are the best. Even today I'd like to suggest to Michael that he buy a left-handed driver for his golf bag just to keep his right-handed clubs on their best behavior. He's a good right-handed golfer now, but he may be even better swinging left-handed.

One beautiful summer day about fourteen years ago, I had the opportunity to talk with the marvelous former Cub, Ron Santo, at Wrigley field in Chicago. I think the Cubs were playing the Giants on this day. I spotted Ron Santo talking with some players near the dugout. When he headed upstairs toward the booth, I asked him if I could have just a minute of his time. He was very cordial and said, "Absolutely." I told him I was planning to write a book sometime soon and that I'd appreciate asking him a few questions. Then I briefly explained the "eyedness concept" to him and asked him if he'd mind taking the quick test. He cordially agreed and he proved to be left-eyed, just what I'd expect from an excellent right-handed hitter and excellent third baseman. Ron's lifetime batting average his fourteen years as a Cub was .279. Add to this that he was an excellent fielding third baseman who could play well off the line and still get the hot line drive grounder down the line. His left-eyedness was very helpful as he moved toward the foul line.

Many of our very best major league baseball players, both past and present, have probably found their correct side swing through experimentation and practice. Probably, however, many excellent athletes who dreamed of playing in the big leagues never made it because they never discovered their correct side swing. Have you? Since pitchers are really not counted on to be excellent hitters, I would guess that many of them today are swinging from their incorrect side. How much better would national league teams be if all of these pitchers batted from the correct side? Most right-handed pitchers would bat from the left-hand batter's box.

Hitting a baseball or softball is not something to be easily coached by others. It is mostly self-taught and improved primarily from the correct side. Excellent coaches should help players find that correct side. Each player can then determine, with some coaching guidance, the best and most comfortable batting stance. Then see the ball in the strike zone and hit it.

My suggestion to each of you is to not be concerned with statistics of the past about what others have done or will do in the future. Rather, focus on what you should do and what you could do to help others find the correct side swing. Then practice enough to make it really work. Let's talk about you and get you to the correct side. You'll also be a more convincing coach if you can demonstrate success in your own past.

If possible, use Wiffle balls in your own backyard. Work on this with your friends. Encourage a friend to swing from his or her correct side. If you discover through your ocular test that you have been swinging from your correct side, simply continue that good process. Know that you should simply practice more diligently to achieve greater success. This quickly builds confidence when you know you are batting from your correct side.

The great golfer, Ben Hogan, once said, "The more I practice the luckier I get." Once you find your correct side, practice that way full speed ahead. No more doubting, just improving with practice, knowing you are hitting from your correct side. This will add enjoyment to your practice time.

You may even want to purchase a Wiffle ball pitching machine and practice by yourself in your own backyard. I have a Wiffle ball pitching machine powered by flashlight batteries. I purchased it for less than fifty dollars.

Here is another suggestion for one of you entrepreneurs. Build and sell a better pitching machine. The machine I use can be loaded with only twelve Wiffle balls, then turn it on and step away and hit the balls as the machine delivers them. Hit the balls from your correct side please. A small backyard is enough to handle this. I know one of you great entrepreneurs out there can design a Wiffle ball pitching machine of far better quality, one of greater capacity and greater reliability. Design it to deliver curveballs also.

Just yesterday, I went to three very prominent sporting goods stores in the Chicago area. My purpose was to see if salespeople at any of the stores knew much about wooden baseball bats. Of the four salespeople I talked with, not one was absolutely certain how to hold a wooden bat, that is, with the trademark facing the batter. Each of these young people had used aluminum bats in their playing days and three of the four young men saw no good reason to face the trademark while hitting so as not to break the bat. The fourth young man, however, noted that the bat probably would not break as easily if the ball was hit on the close grained part of the bat. He was correct. The main purpose for the trademark on all wooden bats is to direct the hitter how to hold the bat. The trademark should face the hitter.

Remember when I mentioned earlier in this book that I have observed several major league players who have held bats incorrectly? If the batter hits the ball well with the trademark not facing the batter, the bat will usually break and the ball will not travel as far as it would have if the batter had held the bat with the trademark facing squarely toward the eyes of the batter. Even though most of our young precollege teams are using aluminum bats today that can be held without regard for the trademark, I feel that it would be excellent to establish that good habit. Most colleges and all professional teams still use the wooden bat. Establish good habits early. Aluminum bats have trademarks for your practice.

Young players who swing from the correct side beginning in early childhood have an excellent chance to play on their schools' varsity baseball or softball teams. Parents and coaches should encourage kids to swing from the correct side very early. Remember Grandma Jan? She encouraged little Robbie to hit the nerf balls back to her right-handed when he was only three. Even though Robbie wanted to

WHAT YOU SEE IS WHAT YOU HIT

try hitting them back left-handed also, Grandma Jan insisted that he continue hitting the nerf balls his very successful way, right-handed. Best athletes in all sports recognize that correct habits established early, then practiced diligently, usually produce best results.

And now a time out to observe the importance of one terrific gentleman and baseball player, who so recently passed away. That's the fabulous "Let's Play Two" Ernie Banks. His excellence as a baseball player for the Chicago Cubs, his genuine beauty as a person to be admired by young and old, his intense enthusiasm for baseball, life, true friendship, and best sportsmanship will keep him in our memories for many years.

Stan Musial gave the eyedness test to Ernie Banks in 1959 and reported to me that he was "solidly left-eyed." This did not surprise me. He absolutely had to be left-eyed. He was excellent right-handed hitter.

As I continue to receive an increasing stream of positive feedback from coaches, players, former students, and friends who have taken the eyedness test and applied it to their own experiences, my excitement and determination to provide you with a helpful guide increases. This book, *What You See Is What You Hit*, is my answer and your guide.

There will always be new things that grasp our attention or old things that are discovered anew and put into practice when the time seems right. The time seems just right to me for people to better understand ocular dominance or eyedness. Let's apply these principles wherever improvement can be achieved in any sport or on any roadway of life.

Let's just keep it simple. Right-eyed baseball and fast-pitch softball players should bat left-handed and left-eyed players should bat right-handed.

Batter up. Correct side please!

The End

Denison University

D

This is to certify that

Arthur Kleck

Has been awarded the Varsity **D** in

Baseball - 1951; 1952; 1953.
Baseball - Co Cap't. 1953.

COACH
COACH
COACH
COACH
COACH

PRESIDENT   DIRECTOR OF ATHLETICS

Oct. 7, 2006
Kleck - middle
Art's induction into his High School Hall of Fame in Archbold, Ohio

The Author's 50th Class Reunion in 2003

Here is the class photo for the front of your 50th **Reunion Memory Book**. We hope you enjoy matching the faces to the memories.

The Alumni Affairs Staff,
Sandy, Susan, Jeanne, Jenny, and Cathy

Class of 1953
Golden 50th Reunion
May 29-June 1, 2003
Photo ID List

Row 1/Floor: John Ames, Morrie Halvorsen, Bob Reid, Robert Campbell, Elaine Vellacott McNiven, Peg Malpass Goddard, Kay Dodge Hansen, John Billingsley, Nancy Redman Barnes, Dick Barnes, Ken Bassett, Corky Lakin, Emilie Connor Vest, Averill Goodrich Young.

Row 2/Seated: Bob DeVore, Martha Wiseley Loy, Judy Berthold Feid, Whitey Broughton, Winifred Woods Gulyas, Eljee Young Bentley, Jo Anne Johnson Trow, Helen Hill Mittnight, JoAnn Hawkins Queenan, Nancy Bimel Heldman, Ann Loehnert Kitzmiller, Betty Young Goodridge, Anne Powell Riley, Florida Fisher Parker, Nancy Friel Stocker, Sallie Pope Schleder, Marilyn Grove DuBois, Jacquie Sovulewski Walker, Jean Hebel Perriman, Maggie Harbaugh Bennett.

Row 3: Pat Wade Zillig, Ardie Dale Zoppel, Mary Elva Congleton Erf, Marcia Rouse Haynes, Jane Davis Ferger, John Crosby, Ann Kinney Throop, Bambi Nelson Williams, Ruth D. Borgeson Elliott.

Row 4: Jacquie Dutro Jaquith, H. William Isaly, Constance Clark Jones, Phyl Schulte Sheehan, Roger Owen, Patricia Murray Owen, Bob Laird, Blitz Creager, Dean Owen, Salli MacSwords Chamberlin, Gerry Granfield Hansen, Jane McCallister Porter, Edith Hartwig Snead, Ruthie Grabeman Widman, Barbara Peters Mosher, Patricia Rolt-Wheeler Robins, Endrik Noges, Joan Harper Van Camp, Margaret Waggoner Wahls, Joyce Duncan Siebens, Nancy Leith Shorney, Richard Gerle.

Row 5: Jim McFarland, Elizabeth Withers Boers, David Kohl, Joan Bowman Craig, Bob Craig, Carl Murray, John Stephen.

Row 6: Jamie Moore, Betty Bevier Ames, Art Kleck, Nancy Brelsford Bourdeau, Gener Guthridge Littell, Dottie Altemeier Morse, Ruth Wooden Roudebush, Charles Hess, Ray Bartlett, John Hutson, Bob Hilberts, Wallace Dunbar, H.A. "Mike" Rosene, Tom McGranahan, Ed Baker, Edward Weber, George Dallas, Ed Boon, Tom Elleman, Guy Glenn, Dick Haid, David Fullmer, Herb Brown, Al Sheahen.

Row 7: Ned Thomson, Mil Curtis Agnor, Nancy Nussbaum Andrews, Mary Jane Chenoweth Thomson, Jack McQuigg, Joseph Sheets, Betty Jaquith Patterson, M.L. Croslin Guerrero, Ruth Wickenden Abel, Jean Ecker Sessions.

A snapchat of Cassidy Wyse taken at a family reunion in Archbold Ohio

Cassidy Wyse - The .511 hitter and niece noted in Art's book

Art Kleck - The Author Principal of West Campus
Lake Forest, Illinois High School
1971-1983

About the Author

Following graduation from Archbold, Ohio High School in 1949, Art attended Denison University in Granville, Ohio. He graduated from Denison in 1953 and was inducted into the United States Army where he served for two years.

He began his teaching career at Swanton High School in Ohio where he taught science and coached varsity baseball and freshman basketball. After two years at Swanton, he joined the Delta, Ohio High School District where he taught science and coached varsity baseball and varsity basketball.

In 1960, Art and his family moved to Lake Forest, Illinois, where he taught German and biology. He coached football and basketball at Lake Forest High School during his teaching years.

In 1971, he was named principal of the new Lake Forest High School West Campus. He remained in that position until West Campus closed in 1983 due to declining enrollment. All students were moved back to the parent East Campus where Art served as dean of students until his retirement from Lake Forest High School in 1986.

In the summer of 1986 Art began his second career as a residential real estate salesperson. Writing this book remained on his "bucket list" until 2014 when he retired. Art said, "Once I retired in 2014, writing the book was a leisurely and enjoyable process."

Today he lives in Libertyville, Illinois with his beloved wife, Barbara.

CPSIA information can be obtained
at www.ICGtesting.com
Printed in the USA
LVHW012257300419
616183LV00005B/59/P

9 781633 387683